SHE WORE A GINGHAM PARTY DRESS THAT COULDN'T HIDE THE SWELL OF HER BREASTS

Celia Kaster stood there indignantly.

"I wasn't sure you'd recognize me with clothes on," Fargo said, and saw the faint flush spread across her cheeks.

"Your methods are inexcusable," she snapped. "Running around half-naked, pretending to be a Crow warrior."

Skye Fargo shrugged. "As I told you, Celia, honey, you were lucky I wasn't the real thing or you'd have a big Crow buck on top of you right now." But he quickly shut up because he could see Celia's eyes hungrily devour his bronzed muscular body. . . .

**ARROWHEAD TERRITORY
THE TRAILSMAN #14**

THE TRAILSMAN 14

ARROWHEAD TERRITORY

by
Jon Sharpe

A SIGNET BOOK

NEW AMERICAN LIBRARY

TIMES MIRROR

PUBLISHER'S NOTE

This novel is a work of fiction. Names, characters, places, and incidents are either the product of the author's imagination or are used fictitiously, and any resemblance to actual persons, living or dead, events, or locales is entirely coincidental.

NAL BOOKS ARE AVAILABLE AT QUANTITY DISCOUNTS WHEN USED TO PROMOTE PRODUCTS OR SERVICES. FOR INFORMATION PLEASE WRITE TO PREMIUM MARKETING DIVISION, THE NEW AMERICAN LIBRARY, INC., 1633 BROADWAY, NEW YORK, NEW YORK 10019.

Copyright © 1982, 1983 by Jon Sharpe

The first chapter of this book appeared in *Blood Chase*, the thirteenth volume of this series.

Ⓞ

SIGNET TRADEMARK REG. U.S. PAT. OFF. AND FOREIGN COUNTRIES
REGISTERED TRADEMARK—MARCA REGISTRADA
HECHO EN CHICAGO, U.S.A.

SIGNET, SIGNET CLASSICS, MENTOR, PLUME, MERIDIAN AND NAL BOOKS are published by The New American Library, Inc., 1633 Broadway, New York, New York 10019

First Printing, February, 1983

1 2 3 4 5 6 7 8 9

PRINTED IN THE UNITED STATES OF AMERICA

The Trailsman

Beginnings . . . they bend the tree and they mark the man. Skye Fargo was born when he was eighteen. Terror was his midwife, vengeance his first cry. Killing spawned Skye Fargo, ruthless, cold-blooded murder. Out of the acrid smoke of gunpowder still hanging in the air, he rose, cried out a promise never forgotten.

The Trailsman, they began to call him, all across the West: searcher, scout, hunter, the man who could see where others only looked, his skills for hire but not his soul, the man who lived each day to the fullest, yet trailed each tomorrow. Skye Fargo, the Trailsman, the seeker who could take the wildness of a land and the wanting of a woman and make them his own.

Some called it the savage land,
some the untamed wilderness.
Those who knew it best called it
Crow country, a land whose
boundaries were marked by arrowheads.

1

Four uniformed soldiers and a young woman with hair of wheat, and, on the ridge above where they rode, the figure lay crouched, watching, clad only in breechclout and headband, black hair falling back away from a chiseled face. The late-afternoon sun tinted his bronzed figure a deep red-gold. His powerful shoulder muscles rippled as he rose onto his haunches and his eyes continued to track the riders below. He had paced the party for almost a mile. They headed for Sunwater and Fort Jasper, he knew.

The bronzed figure almost smiled as he thought of Fort Jasper. He understood why some laughed at it. No major line fort such as Kearny or Peck or Union, it was but a small army compound that sat at the edge of Crow country like a lonely frog on a huge lake. Yet the white man kept coming to try to settle on the land and looked for protection to the officers and men of Fort Jasper. The powerful, bronzed figure rose to his feet and trotted to his horse waiting back from the top of the ridgeline. He swung on the horse's back, felt the warmth of the pinto's body through his legs, and moved down from the ridge.

Fort Jasper was too far to reach by nightfall, and the riders below would halt to make camp for the night, he knew. He watched the dusk creep in purple streaks across the land, good, rich, fertile land, land full of bear and moose, white-tailed deer and rich beaver. The Crow land was the best land. It had everything one could want, and the Crow had no mind to share it with anyone. The other tribes had learned that, and the white man was learning it, too.

The riders came into view, veering off into a small glen beside a stream that ran slowly and almost silently. The tall, powerful figure slowed, watched the stream move into the glen, traced its passage with his eyes. It wandered down from the hills, edged the glen, and moved on. He spurred his horse down closer to the uniformed soldiers and the girl with the wheat hair, dismounted to watch as she washed in the stream. Her skin gleamed as she moistened her face and arms, down across her neck and collarbone. She wore a black riding skirt, and her breasts were deep beneath a light-blue shirt. He'd enjoyed the way they swayed in unison as she rode.

He edged closer, leading the horse. It was growing dark quickly, and the soldiers had lighted a very small fire. The girl with the wheat hair was someone special, he knew, by the way the soldiers treated her. She was no camp girl they took their pleasure with, embraced as they pleased. She stayed by herself, ate alone, shared a biscuit with the men, and finally lay down under her blanket. He watched the soldiers set up two sentries in the little glen as the night grew black. Content to wait and watch, he saw they had tethered their horses together. A mistake, he grunted, always a mistake.

The powerful, near-naked figure leaned against a tree and let the night grow long. The moon rose, a dim moon, and he saw the soldiers were taking two-hour sentry shifts. He nodded in approval. It let them stand sentry and yet get ample sleep. Finally the muscled figure rose,

2

and moved with easy grace, eyes scanning the glen again. It was a half-circle with the stream bordering the one side, but the brush and trees around it were heavy. It would be difficult to move through them without rustling a branch or cracking a twig. But there were ways to prevent that, and the tall, bronzed figure circled to where the stream coursed down the hill to the glen. He left the horse beside a tree and stepped into the stream, moved down it with absolute noiselessness, risking no stray twig to crack underfoot, no thick bushes to rustle like the gingham skirts the white women wore. The water felt cool and refreshing around his ankles and he neared the glen, silent as a wraith.

The dim moon outlined the little camp, and the horses came into sight on the other side of the glen. The small fire was little more than embers now, and he lowered himself into a crouch, continued to move forward in the stream. He was abreast of the two sentries now, both men with their backs to him. The soft call of a horned lark drifted through the stillness. He moved past the sentries with the sound of the stream, halted at the horses, and stepped from the water.

He drew a knife from the waistband of his breechclout, cut the horses loose, stepped back, and pricked the rump of the nearest one with the tip of the knifeblade. The horse let out a cry of surprise more than pain, reared up, and bolted. The others went with him at once, and the bronzed figure stood back in the trees, watched the soldiers racing after the fleeing animals. Two men splashed along the stream after the mounts while the other two raced through the woods to try to drive them back.

The girl was sitting up and she pushed herself to her feet, clothed in a slip that did little to hold back the deep, soft line of creamy breasts. She reached for her shirt, pulled it over herself, and the bronzed figure moved on silent feet, appeared before her as though he'd dropped from the sky. He saw the girl's eyes widen, fear and something more as she stared at the magnificent figure before her. Her scream tore the night when he reached down and scooped her up as one might scoop up a child, with effortless ease, threw her over one shoulder, and raced up to where he had left the horse.

"Stop," he heard her scream. "Help, dammit . . . over here!" He felt her fists pound against his back and then her nails dig into him, and he felt the pain of her marks. He shook her hard, and she yelped. Two of the soldiers had stopped trying to catch the horses and were running after him. But he had reached his horse, and he flung the wheat-haired girl atop it, swung up beside her, and raced through the forest. He held the reins with his arms around her waist as she sat the horse in front of him, and he felt the warm softness of her breasts against his skin. She smelled good, too, powder and some kind of oil. He sent the horse veering across the slope, rode hard, not that they were close behind. He couldn't even hear their shouts anymore.

He rode, followed the hillside downward until he reached the flatland below, and enjoyed the softness of her buttocks against his flat, bronzed belly. He reined to a halt, swung from the horse, and lifted her down to the ground with one arm. She backed, watched his beautifully muscled form leap from the pinto. "Don't you touch me," she warned as he stood before her, hands on his hips. He laughed, a deep, rich sound, and saw her eyes were unable to look away from the magnificence of his near-naked body. He lifted his eyes from her to see the pink of the new day staining the night sky. He sat down, cross-legged, thumped a hand on the ground, and she lowered herself across from him. He made no motion toward her, let his eyes enjoy the beauty of her, and she buttoned the

4

shirt as high as she could. It only served to press the shape of her breasts tighter against the fabric. She had a nice nose, slightly upturned, and in the growing dawn he saw she had round cheeks, a pretty face that held just a touch of arrogance, light-brown eyes.

He saw her frowning at him, knew she was confused as much as frightened, now. Her eyes continued to move across his body, and it was with an effort that she focused on the handsomeness of his intense, chiseled face. The new day came to give everything new definition, and the tall figure rose, stood over the girl. She gazed up at him, saw him smile, and the frown began to slide across her smooth forehead, stayed, dug in deeper.

"You can get up," the tall, bronzed figure said.

The girl's lips fell open and she began to pull herself to her feet. He reached a hand out and helped her up. He saw her staring at his eyes, the dawn revealing the brilliant lake-blue color. "You're no Indian," she gasped. "Not with those eyes."

"Didn't say I was," the man answered.

"What in hell is this? Who are you?" she asked, her eyes still wearing astonishment.

"Fargo . . . Skye Fargo," he said.

2

He watched a stampede of emotions race inside her light-brown eyes, astonishment, anger, disbelief, wariness. "If this is supposed to be a joke it isn't funny," she said icily.

"No joke," Fargo remarked blandly.

Her eyes narrowed, studying his face. "No joke," she repeated, and he saw the anger rise to push the other emotions aside inside her eyes. "You're just some kind of crazy that goes around playing Indian and scaring people to death," she said, a furrow creasing her smoothly rounded forehead.

"Not usually," he said.

"Then what in God's name is all this?" she flung back.

Fargo let a small smile edge his lips. "Research," he said and saw her eyebrows shoot skyward.

"Research?" she exploded. "What kind of answer is that?"

"Better than you know," Fargo said. "How do you rate a cavalry escort to Sunwater?"

She drew haughtiness around herself. "I was on my way to visit my uncle, who happens to be Colonel Henry Kaster, commander of Fort Jasper," she said.

Fargo's heavy, black brows lifted. "No shit," he said and then laughed as she watched incredulously.

"Dammit, who are you, Fargo? I demand an explanation for all this," she snapped.

"Ask Uncle Henry." Fargo grinned as he turned, swung himself onto the pinto with one easy motion. "Your soldier boys are out looking for you," he said. "And getting sick and scared by the minute. I'll see they find you." He reached a hand down and she took it. He lifted her onto the pinto in front of him as though she were a child. Her soft rear came to rest against him, and he knew she couldn't help but feel the bulk of his warm male potency through the thin breechclout. She tried to move forward but, sitting astride the pinto's withers, it was impossible and she had to slide back against him. He moved the horse forward, grinned as he felt her tenseness. His powerful arms brushed the soft sides of her breasts as he reached past her to pull lightly on the reins. He spotted the four troopers on the slope below, spread out, trying to make a sweep of the area.

"Here's where you get off," Fargo said to the girl. "They'll be along in a few minutes." He swung from the pinto and helped her down, grinned at her as she stared at him, the light-brown eyes full of exasperated disbelief.

"I still think I'm dreaming all this," she muttered.

He reached out, pulled her to him, held her against the warmth of his muscled nakedness. "Still think so?" he asked.

She swallowed, pressed her palms against the smoothness of his chest, and he let her step back. "No," she said, her voice small, then finding anger at once. "And you haven't heard the end of this, whoever or whatever you are," she said.

"I imagine not," Fargo said dryly. "Just consider yourself lucky."

"Lucky?" She frowned.

"I could have been a real Crow warrior," he said, his

voice suddenly cold, and he saw the moment of realization touch her eyes. The four troopers had started up the slope, and Fargo turned the pinto. "The colonel's niece has to have a name," he said.

"Celia Wright," she answered, and he nodded at her, then sent the pinto racing away to disappear over the crest of the slope. He sent a harsh laugh into the wind as he rode alone. The colonel's niece, he reflected silently. All hell would break loose now. Not that it mattered any longer. The time for preparing was about over, Fargo pondered, the lake-blue eyes growing cold. He crested another rise alongside a line of red ash, reined to a halt as he saw the two riders a dozen yards in front of him. Damn, he cursed silently as the two men focused on him. Two drifters. He's seen them all day yesterday as they tried to pick up his trail and he'd easily outmaneuvered them, but now they'd suddenly grown lucky. He saw them wheel their horses at once, start for him.

Drifters. Troublemakers. It was in their stubbled faces, the mean-dog look of them. They were overjoyed for the chance at a lone Crow warrior, and he saw one of the men pull a rifle from a saddle holster. Fargo swerved the pinto into the forest of red ash, glanced back to see the two drifters racing after him, evil anticipation in their rock-scrabble faces. He grunted, bitterness in the sound. He'd oblige them, become what they sought, a Crow warrior again, and he sent the pinto deeper into the woodland. He pressed himself low on the horse's back and saw the brush underfoot grow thick, made for concealment. A tight smile touched his face, but he didn't dive from the pinto. Instead, long, powerful arms shot upward, hands wrapping around a tree branch, and the bronzed figure vanished into the foliage. Fargo clung to the branch, drew his legs around it, became motionless in an instant as the pinto ran on a few yards and came to a halt.

The two drifters rode into the forest of red ash, both now holding rifles, Fargo saw. Their eyes scanned the woods and spotted the pinto. The taller man nudged the other. "He's trying to hide out in the brush," he said. "We'll flush him out like a damn prairie dog."

The two men moved forward slowly, rifles ready, their eyes sweeping the brush on both sides. The bronzed figure lay motionless on the branch, watching with contempt. They were fools. He could kill them both with ease, and he wondered if he should do so. The Crow warrior they thought they had trapped would kill them both and laugh. He held the thought a moment longer and then let it go. It was enough that he had first thought as the Crow, knew what the Crow would do and how he'd do it. He let his powerful leg muscles relax, his legs unwrap from around the branch. The two men were almost directly underneath him, eyes peering down and forward at the brush.

Fargo stiffened his body, tightened every muscle from neck to feet, and dropped from the branch with his body horizontal, arms pushed forward rigidly. He smashed into both riders at once as though he were a pole dropped onto them. Their shouts were made of pain and surprise as they toppled from their horses. Once he had struck the two men, Fargo relaxed the rigidness of his body and landed on the ground on all fours. He was on his feet spinning around as the two drifters were still shaking their heads, sprawled on the ground. The nearest man had started to rise to his feet when Fargo's blow, delivered at the end of a long, sweeping arc, smashed him into the ground. The second man had recovered enough to try to dive forward at the bronzed figure. Fargo's kick caught him full in the stomach as he came forward.

"Agh . . . Jesus," the man gasped, clutching both hands to his abdomen as he pitched forward, his face contorted in pain. Fargo brought his heavy fist down on the back of the man's neck with a tremendous blow, and the figure went limp, hands still pressed to his midsection. Fargo rose, stared down at the two men for a moment. Once again, he felt the moment's urge to carry out his role, felt his hand move toward the hunting knife at his waist. But once again he let the moment pass away. More and more he was realizing how uncomfortably thin was the line between knowing the savage and being the savage.

He turned from the two inert forms, whistled softly, and the pinto trotted toward him. He swung onto the horse and rode away. The two drifters would wake in time and make up their own stories about why they still had their scalps. Fargo rode out of the woodland and across the slope, upward to a small pool tucked away in the hills. He dismounted and stripped the breechclout off and stepped into the cool water, sank all of himself down, floated lazily, and then ducked his head under to surface again after a moment, the red-bronze skin color washing away. It had been a mixture of dyes, marigold and the red taken from the female cochineal beetle, which the Indians usually used undiluted. As the tinted water drifted away, he emerged to stand naked in the sun, his body tanned but no longer bronzed. He reached under a flat stone and pulled out a towel, his clothes, and the gunbelt with the big Colt .45 in the holster. He dried himself, dressed leisurely, and lay down beside the pool. The body demanded the replenishment only sleep could bring, and he closed his eyes under the warm yellow blanket.

It was an afternoon sky when he woke. He stretched, rose, climbed onto the pinto, and slowly turned the horse toward Sunwater.

Fort Jasper stood at the west end of Sunwater, the town stretching out behind it in a long, narrow line. It was termed a fort, but it was more truly a glorified stockade with only one blockhouse. Inside its less-than-sturdy compound, the voice of Colonel Henry Kaster boomed through his living quarters, which were attached to the regiment offices.

"The sonofabitch went too far this time," the colonel thundered. He paused to take a drink from the glass in his hand and cast an angry glance at his wife, who sat across from him. Martha Kaster made no comment, her full figure more than filling the narrow wooden chair. She ran one hand over her hair, still mostly brown with but a few strands turning gray. "You hear me, Martha? He's gone too far this time," the colonel said.

Martha Kaster nodded coolly, her dark-brown eyes holding on her husband as he paced back and forth across the room. His face was flushed, she noted, but then his face was almost always flushed, just as the glass of gin and lemon juice was almost always in his hand. Colonel Henry Kaster's half-buttoned uniform hung loosely on a thin, bony frame, and his hand shook ever so slightly as he put the glass to his lips again.

"My own niece," he thundered. "Terrifying the poor girl, turning her trip into a nightmare. All because of his damnfool game-playing ridiculousness. Well, I'll have no more of it. The big bastard's done it this time."

"Is that all you're furious about, Henry?" Martha Kaster said, getting to her feet, large breasts tightening the bodice of her maroon dress. "Because he scared Celia half to death?"

The colonel stared at his wife with almost colorless eyes, his flushed face frowning. "What are you saying in that goddamn sideways way of yours, Martha?" he flung at her.

Martha Kaster had learned to wear impassiveness the way most women wear clothes. Only her words speared.

11

"It seems to me that he did demonstrate, rather effectively, that Celia could well have been in a Crow camp now," she said.

"Goddammit, you making excuses for what he did?" the colonel roared. "You on his side?"

"No, dear, I'm on your side," Martha Kaster said. "But I think you've handled this entire business very poorly. You should have brought him around to your way of thinking instead of being antagonistic."

"No goddamn civilian's going to tell me I can't catch a stinking Indian, no matter what damn general sent him," Colonel Kaster bellowed and finished his drink. He pushed the empty glass at his wife. "Fix me another," he growled.

"Remember, Henry, you're to escort Celia and me to the harvest hoedown tonight," Martha Kaster said as she took the glass.

"I'll be perfectly sober. Just fix the damn drink," the colonel growled.

Martha Kaster held her comment inside herself. Sober was a relative term with Henry Kaster, she grunted inwardly. She went to a sideboard, poured the gin from a crystal decanter, the lemon juice from an ironware pitcher. "Please, Henry, no scene tonight if Fargo shows up," she said, handing her husband the refilled glass.

Henry Kaster fastened her with his colorless eyes. "Don't tell me how to behave," he muttered.

Martha maintained her calm impassiveness. "It's just that everyone looks forward all summer to the harvest hoedown. Let's not spoil it," she said.

"I'm not going to spoil their goddamn hoedown. I'm letting them use the compound, aren't I?" The colonel glowered.

"Yes, as always, and that's very good of you, Henry," Martha said soothingly. As the colonel turned from her to

12

take a long pull of his drink, she walked into the bedroom and pushed the door closed behind her. She sank down on the big double bed with the heavy oak headboard and lay back in the dim light of the curtained windows. Almost instantly, the big, black-haired man with the intense, lake-blue eyes swam into her thoughts. He'd been there too often since he had come to Sunwater, and Martha Kaster silently cursed his presence. For more than one reason, she reminded herself.

To her husband, he was an insult, salt on an open wound. To her he was a danger and a reminder, a danger to her future and a reminder of all she had worked so hard to put aside in her life. Either way, she would have to deal with the man they called the Trailsman, Martha Kaster had already decided.

Just thinking about him brought on its own set of problems, Martha conceded silently. She had watched his eyes, penetrating, full of inner knowing, a man of wild-creature acuteness. There'd be no fooling his kind, not with words or masquerades. Damn the man, she swore softly, suddenly warm, her skin coated with tiny beads of perspiration. She opened the top buttons of her bodice and let her large, soft breasts push free to drink in the air. The half-smile that touched Martha Kaster's lips was made of bitterness. She continued to think of one way above all others. Once, with a man such as Fargo, it would have been only pure pleasure. Now it promised only pain wrapped in a moment of pleasure. But perhaps it was the only way, and Martha Kaster wondered if she really sought another way. Only one fact was certain in her mind. She'd do what had to be done, whatever it was. She couldn't sit idly by and watch Fargo destroy her tomorrows. Too many trapped, sterile years had paid for them, too many.

Martha Kaster closed her eyes to nap before it came time to dress for the evening's festivities.

The town of Sunwater lay astride the triangle where the Dakota Territory met Montana and Wyoming, neither place yet ranking as a territory, much less a state. An oasis in the very center of Crow country, it took its name from the small lake along one edge of town that reflected the first rays of the morning sun. Night had lowered as Fargo rode into town, a low-hanging harvest moon looking almost unreal in its perfect roundness. He saw the lanterns being strung inside the compound at the fort as he rode by the open gates and headed down the single street that was the town of Sunwater.

He halted outside the frame structure with the wooden sign that proclaimed BOARDERS, dismounted, and stepped into the house. The young woman inside looked up at him, just as she had that evening three weeks ago when he'd arrived, but the astonishment didn't flood her eyes this time. Nor his as he regarded Patricia Rooney, took in the heavy flatiron on the board in front of her with the white party blouse. Patty Rooney's gray-blue eyes met his studied appraisal.

"What are you thinking?" she asked.

"What I thought that night three weeks back," Fargo said. "How little you've changed in five years." His eyes traveled down over her shoulders, bare except for the thin straps of her undergarment, her slightly long breasts softly shaped under the cotton. Patty Rooney had a face more pleasant than pretty, plain features framed by medium-brown hair she wore back in a pigtail. But she had a generous mouth quick to laugh and eyes that carried their own quiet sultriness, a long-waisted body with flat hips and legs muscled yet shapely.

"You did it this time, Fargo," Patty Rooney said. "It's all over town. Did you have to pick the colonel's niece?"

Fargo allowed a short laugh. "I didn't pick her. It just turned out that way," he said, glanced at the white blouse beside the triangular flatiron. "Going to go to the hoedown with me?" he asked, grinning at her.

Her glance was mock severity. "You know the answer to that, Fargo. I don't want to start any gossip. You're just a boarder. Nobody knows we go back to before I married Ted. I've run the place without gossip since Ted was killed last year, and I want to keep it that way. I don't want any questions, nobody finding out I once worked in a dancehall."

"Hell, you were no whore," Fargo protested.

"Some folks think any gal that works in a dancehall has got to be a whore. You know that," Patty answered.

Fargo conceded the truth in her words with a nod. His hand reached out to stroke her hair. "Finding you here in Sunwater's been the only good thing about this town," he said. "We should turn the clock back, Patty." His hand moved down along the back of her neck to the soft skin there, covered gently by the fine hairs of her neck.

She leaned her bare shoulders back against him. "I'm afraid, Fargo. I'll want it to stay turned back, and I know that can't happen."

"You stop looking at sunsets?" he asked.

She frowned at him. "Of course not. Why do you ask a fool thing like that?"

"They don't last, either," he remarked.

Patty Rooney stared at him for a long moment, and the wry smile slowly touched her lips. "You always had a way with answers," she said, moved away from him to pick up the blouse and walk from the room. She paused in the doorway. "Maybe I'll come back early from the hoedown," she said.

"Maybe I will, too," he said and watched the tiny smile in her eyes as she turned and went into the other room.

Fargo went down the hall to his room, let the lamp stay out as he sank down on the single cot to stretch out. He clasped powerful hands behind his head, closed his eyes, and let thoughts drift back to the meeting that had brought him here to Sunwater. It suddenly seemed so long ago, yet it was hardly a month past. The note had come first, reaching him at the Luther ranch in Ox Hill where he'd delivered a herd of longhorns up from Texas territory. He'd read it with a smile, the contents in the sender's usual brief style, saying a little and a lot at once.

Fargo—
    Special job; special pay; special man.
General Mark Peterson
U.S. Army
Sixth Division

Fargo had rested another day and then taken the journey to the army command post at the edge of the Minnesota border, good memories and curiosity riding with him. He'd ridden beside General Mark Peterson on an army mission, fought cutthroats beside him, and had come to respect and admire the man, an accolade he didn't accord most men.

When he reached the command post the general met him behind closed doors, the tall form still very erect despite a leg filled with bullet lead, the blue uniform making his white hair seem even whiter.

"Glad you came, Fargo," the general said.

"Hell, you knew that note would fetch me," Fargo answered and drew a smile from the long, weathered face. General Mark Peterson's gaze traveled over the big black-haired man in front of him with the experience of years of evaluating men.

"Haven't changed any that I can see," the general said. "That's good." He eased himself into a wooden chair and stretched one leg out in a straight line. "Ever hear of a town called Sunwater?" he asked.

"Heard of it. Never been there. Smack in the middle of Crow country, isn't it?" Fargo said.

"That's right," the general said. "We built Fort Jasper there, one more high-command mistake. Folks came thinking the army would keep their scalps on while they settled their lands."

"Reasonable enough thinking," Fargo commented.

"Reasonable enough, but it hasn't worked that way. My command is spread so thin I don't have an extra cook. Fort Jasper is garrisoned with green troops commanded by Colonel Henry Kaster, a misfit and a boozer who was never much good sober," the general said.

"Why was he given the post?" Fargo asked.

General Peterson turned a jaundiced eye on him. "Hell, Fargo, you know the army. The system is made for covering up. You have a problem, you don't air it out loud. You sweep it into a corner someplace."

"In this case a corner named Fort Jasper," Fargo finished.

The general nodded bitterness. "Washington assigned him, happy to put him off somewhere. The territory is technically under my command, but I'm helpless to make any practical moves and it's all taken a bad turn." He paused as Fargo's brows lifted a notch in question. "There's one very smart or very crazy Indian raising a special kind of hell. He's come up with something different, and he's making it work. He's waged a campaign to take only the women—wives, daughters, sisters, any woman. He calls himself something I'm told roughly

17

translates into Hawkwing. Anyway, that's what he's called."

Fargo let his lips purse for a moment. "It's a different approach, all right," he reflected aloud.

"Different and especially nasty. Some men went after their women and were killed trying. Most have been shattered, unable or unwilling to go on alone. A few still keep hoping. But he's hitting where it hurts the most. Hell, death is always near out here. A man can live with that fact. He can even accept the death of a loved one, wrestle with the grief and find the strength to go on. It's not knowing that does him in. Not knowing is worse than acceptance, worse than grieving. It corrodes the spirit, and right now nobody knows whether the women Hawkwing has taken are dead, shipped away, being held for something else, maybe bargaining, or just being used by every buck in his camp."

"And Colonel Kaster?" Fargo questioned.

"My information is that he keeps sending out patrols to try to catch this damn Crow. Of course, they've gotten nowhere. Hawkwing hits and vanishes. He's let the colonel's troopers wear themselves out chasing shadows. What's more, he hasn't struck at them once."

Fargo's frown echoed the general's lowered brow. "Interesting," he commented.

"You and I both know damn well it's not because he couldn't," the general said. "It's part of whatever the hell he's doing, part of only striking at the women for now. And whatever else he might be planning."

"And Colonel Kaster?"

"The colonel thinks Hawkwing's afraid to take on his troopers."

"The colonel's a damn fool," Fargo grunted.

"Exactly. Neither the colonel nor his men are up to catching this Crow. That's why I sent for you. I want this damned Crow stopped, and I want to find out what's happened to the women he's taken. You're the one man who might be able to do the job. You might just be able to pick up a trail," General Peterson said.

"It'll take a damn sight more than picking up a few signs. This Indian is carefully carrying out his plans. What you want can only be done if I can anticipate his moves. That means I'll have to spend time there, learn the land, see as a Crow, think as a Crow, act as a Crow, become a Crow in everything but name."

General Peterson nodded. "You're the one man who could make it work," he said. "I've a special pay authorization for you, enough to make it worth your while. It'll be sent to you the usual way."

"That helps," Fargo said laconically.

The general took an envelope from the drawer of the desk, handed it to Fargo. "These are my orders to Colonel Kaster, telling him to cooperate with you and why you've been sent."

Fargo's smile was thin. "You think he'll go along with that?" he asked.

"He'll have to, whether he likes it or not. It's an official order," the General said. "But he has one ace in the hole. A field commander has the right to disregard any general order if he feels the immediate situation warrants it. So don't push him too far too fast. Stay out of his hair as much as possible."

"That could be easier said than done," Fargo answered, folding the envelope into a pocket. General Peterson rose, favoring his stiff leg, and extended his hand in a firm clasp.

"Good luck, Fargo," he said. "Keep your scalp on."

That had been the beginning, the task spelled out. He had come to Sunwater and found the unexpected in Patty Rooney's presence and the expected in Colonel Kaster's reception. The man's hand had trembled as he read the order from General Peterson, too much gin as responsible as too much anger, Fargo decided quickly. Martha Kaster had been there at that first meeting in the colonel's quarters, and Fargo had seen how her dark-brown eyes held on him with something more than casual interest, a hint of apprehension as well as appreciation in her face. A tall woman with large, loose breasts, perhaps pushing forty, she was nonetheless attractive, with good, even features, a full mouth, and a simmering sensuousness she kept carefully cloaked.

"He's got his damn nerve sending me an order like this," the colonel had thundered. "This is insulting. I resent his sending you out here very much, you understand that, Fargo? I don't need you to show me how to catch this damn Indian."

"Maybe I can show you why you're not catching him," Fargo answered mildly.

"By trying to be a Crow yourself? That won't catch that redskinned ghost. I'll get him my own way, and this order of Peterson's is just too goddamned insulting," Colonel Kaster returned.

"You saying you're not going to follow the order?" Fargo asked.

He watched the man take a pull of the gin and lemon juice, his thin lips working nervously when he finished. "I don't disobey orders, but General Mark Peterson hasn't heard the end of this," the man said. "And don't expect me to go around looking out for you and your damnfool shenanigans."

"Wouldn't think of it," Fargo said. "Now I want a list of the families he's hit and the women he's taken."

"What the hell good's that going to do you?" the colonel snapped.

"I do things my way, you do them yours. Just give me

the list," Fargo said, and the impatience grew harsh in his voice.

The colonel pulled a desk drawer open, rummaged through it, and handed Fargo a sheet of paper with names written in pencil on it. Fargo glanced at it quickly, folded the paper, and pushed it into his pocket. The colonel took another drink and threw a wave at his wife.

"Martha, show our great Indian fighter out. I've work to do," he said.

Fargo stepped to one side as Martha Kaster led the way to the door of the colonel's quarters, beyond view from inside the room. She held the door open for him, leaned against the frame, and her eyes studied him again.

"I hope you're not as unhappy with me as the colonel is," Fargo remarked.

Her eyes stayed veiled. "Not yet," she said, and Fargo left with a quiet laugh that echoed in her eyes.

And so it had begun, the weeks passing quickly, Fargo reflected as he stretched his big frame the length of the cot. Word of his presence and his mission had spread quickly, in Sunwater and out among those who had settled in a wide perimeter beyond the town and Fort Jasper. He had shown some how they were leaving themselves open to a Crow attack and others how they courted disaster by bad habits. As a Crow warrior in all but name, he delivered object lessons that struck home hard. A few gave only grudging admission, but most were chastened and grateful, and all wondered if he could indeed succeed where Colonel Kaster and his troopers had failed.

In between, Fargo found time to touch base at the little room and to visit the compound, where he saw the colonel's resentment deepening and his consumption of gin increasing. A few times he found the colonel passed out across his desk, and one evening Martha Kaster was there, quietly watching over her husband as one watches over an ill child. She had met Fargo with a combination of resentment and protectiveness laced with the simmering sensuousness that she almost managed to cloak.

"Your being here isn't helping Henry," she said firmly.

"You mean it's giving him more excuses to drink," Fargo corrected.

Her eyes narrowed. "It's easy to be harsh," she said.

"As easy as making excuses," he returned.

"You don't like weakness," she said.

"I don't like waste," he answered.

Her eyes studied him for a moment. "You mean the waste of a good military man?" she probed.

"I mean the waste of a good woman," Fargo returned.

Her eyes stayed on him, and suddenly she was breathing harshly, the large, loose breasts rising and falling in quickened rhythm. But she held her cloak tight around herself, and the figure sprawled face down over the desk suddenly made a guttural sound. Martha Kaster turned. "Goodnight, Fargo. I'm going to help the colonel into bed," she said.

Fargo walked to the door and made no offer to assist. Her dignity would have made her refuse. Besides, she'd plenty of experience at the task, he was certain. He had left and returned to the night and the forest, becoming a Crow warrior again before an hour had passed.

So the weeks went forward, his visits with the colonel and Martha infrequent, his stops at the room he'd rented even more so. Even his exchanges with the settlers were but intermissions. Mostly, he lived in the ways of the wild and did what he had come to do, studied the land, questioned those on the list he had been given, listened, watched, immersed himself in the ways of the red man. He had seen Crow war parties when no one else had seen them and read the signs where no one else could read them. He had come to know the Crow warrior chief in

22

the way one can learn about the fox by watching the henhouse. And finally, now, there was little more to learn this way. The Crow would not hold off striking again, he was certain. The time had come to act.

Fargo heard the sound of the front door opening and being closed firmly. Patty had left for the hoedown. He rose slowly, changed his clothes, and finally left the house to stroll along the dark street toward the compound of the fort. The sounds of the music drifted through the night, and Fargo's eyes narrowed in grimness. As he drew closer to the compound he picked out the sounds of a fiddle, a concertina, and a saw. The sounds of foot-stomping and clapping rose in the air, and he passed a long line of wagons along the outer wall of the compound, mostly buckboards with some pony wagons and runabouts and a few spring wagons.

The soft glow of the kerosene lamps strung on ropes gave the compound a pleasant mellowness. Fargo's glance took in the dancers and the onlookers, the side tables of simple but hearty food, and the big keg of corn whiskey to one side. The keg was doing the briskest business, he saw, with both troopers and settlers on line. He spied Patty in the middle of a Virginia reel and saw her eyes meet his for the briefest of moments. He wandered casually, exchanged words with those settlers he had come to know, and stopped at the keg for a cup of corn spirits. It turned out to be deserving of the term "firewater." He'd strolled forward to watch the dancers take up a Tennessee two-step when he heard the voice at his elbow.

"I wondered if you'd have the poor taste to show up," it said, and he turned to see the girl, her wheat-blond hair hanging below her shoulders, softened in the yellow glow of the lanterns.

"You've got your answer," Fargo said, meeting the frown of her light-brown eyes. She wore a gingham party dress, he noted, full of frills in the front that couldn't hide the swell of her breasts. The dress came in at a small waist, covered a round figure with annoying flounces. "I wasn't sure you'd recognize me with clothes on," Fargo said blandly.

He saw the faint flush spread across her round cheeks. "I know all about you, now, and I agree with my uncle. Your methods are inexcusable," she said.

"But effective," Fargo said mildly. "For those not too stupid or stubborn to learn."

"I presume you're referring to the colonel, because he doesn't go along with you or your mission here," she said with a touch of loftiness.

Fargo half shrugged. "As I told you, Celia, honey, you were lucky I wasn't the real thing or you'd have a big Crow buck on top of you right now."

The color in her cheeks deepened. "You enjoy being crude, I see," she snapped.

"I enjoy being honest," Fargo corrected. "What brings you out here, Celia?"

"Do you know Judy Thompson?" she asked, and Fargo nodded. Judy was the elder of two daughters in the Thompson family. The father, Jed, worked a parcel of land the other side of the lake. "Judy and I were friends back in Pennsylvania, and she wrote and asked me to visit. I got in touch with Uncle and he said to come right out and stay with him and Martha."

"Even sent an escort of troopers to keep you safe," Fargo commented and saw Celia's lips tighten.

"You don't think he should have had me come out at all, do you?" she asked.

"Bull's-eye, sweetie," Fargo snapped. "But he couldn't tell you not to come. That'd be admitting he's not in control of things, and he's too weak to face that."

"That's a terrible thing to say," Celia threw back.

"I could say more. I'm being kind," Fargo told her harshly. He let a smile come to his lips. "But I did enjoy our little ride together," he said.

"I didn't," she snapped.

Fargo's eyes showed his disbelief as his glance went past her to the figure approaching, uniform buttoned properly for a change, his walk steady but his face carrying the red-veined flush of alcohol. Martha Kaster followed a step behind, and in her dark-brown eyes Fargo thought he saw a silent plea for tolerance.

"I hope this man is apologizing to you, Celia," the colonel said, his face drawn in tight. Fargo saw others nearby turn to listen.

"Hardly," Celia answered.

"Then I demand you apologize to my niece here and now, Fargo," the colonel said to the big man in front of him.

"I'd say you ought to do the apologizing, colonel, seeing as how the soldier boys you picked didn't exactly keep her safe," Fargo said, his voice mild. He saw the colonel's mouth tremble in fury.

"Dammit, Fargo, I've had it with you. I don't care what General Peterson ordered. One more move like that last one and I'll lock you up," the colonel thundered.

"Save your breath, colonel," Fargo said, his voice suddenly cold. "The time for preparing is done with. I'll be going out after Hawkwing and the women soon."

He saw the sneer begin to slide across the colonel's face. "So the Trailsman is ready to make his move, is he?" the man said, sarcasm flooding his voice. "We might just be seeing the last of you."

Fargo's smile was thin. "Not exactly a vote of confidence, is it?" he said.

"You're damn right it's not," the colonel boomed. "I'll be taking care of that Crow and the safety of folks around here, just as I'm doing tonight." Fargo let his eyebrows lift in question, watched the colonel sweep those looking on with a self-satisfied glance. "Three troopers will be escorting each wagon home from the hoedown. After drinking and dancing, folks are bound to be relaxed, their guard down. It'd be just like that Crow to strike now, but I'm going to see that everybody gets home safely."

The colonel smiled at the murmur of approval that rose from those listening, and Fargo saw a woman hurry off, immediately spreading the word about the escort. The colonel turned to him. "Nothing to say, Fargo?" he asked waspishly.

Fargo's chiseled face remained expressionless. "Nope," he said.

Colonel Kaster held on to his sneer. "Folks will see that I'm more than capable of keeping them safe," he said. "Let's go on, Martha." He started to walk off, paused to beckon to Celia. "Come along, my dear," he said.

"In a moment. I'll catch up with you," the girl answered, and the colonel strode off. Fargo saw Martha Kaster glance back at him, a tiny furrow on her brow. He felt Celia Wright's eyes on him, met her studied appraisal. "Go on, say it," she pushed at him.

"Say what?" he asked innocently.

"What you didn't say to the colonel just now," she snapped.

Fargo considered for a moment, half shrugged. "The trooper escort's a waste of time," he commented.

"Why?" she questioned sharply.

"Hawkwing won't strike at any wagons tonight," Fargo said almost idly.

"What makes you so sure?" Celia pressed.

"He knows that's what the Colonel expects, and he

26

won't do the expected. Besides, he's never made a night attack. That's not his way," Fargo said.

Celia's brow lowered angrily.

"Why didn't you tell the colonel that?" she asked.

Fargo's eyes narrowed. "Because he wouldn't have listened."

Celia's lips tightened in a moment of silent admission. "Maybe this Hawkwing doesn't even know there's a harvest hoedown," she said with hopefulness.

"He knows," Fargo grunted.

Celia continued to study the big man. "When do you think he'll strike again?" she asked.

Fargo let his face take on a pained grimace. "If I knew that, I'd be there," he said roughly. "He's got too many options. I know only one thing. It'll be the unexpected time, the best time in his eyes."

A faint shudder passed through Celia's body, and her eyes lost the anger in them as she looked at Fargo. "How can you, one man, expect to stop him?" she asked. "I agree with my uncle. It's ridiculous."

"Maybe," Fargo said.

"I still think an apology is in order," she said.

"You don't have to apologize. I'll forgive you," he smiled affably and saw her jaw drop, exasperation start to flood her face. She was still sputtering as he strolled away.

"Crude!" he heard her call after him as he stopped at the keg and downed another cup of the corn spirits. He watched Celia as she walked away, wheat hair soft under the yellow lantern glow, her rear swinging nicely beneath the flounces of the dress. It was too bad he'd not more time to spend with Celia Wright, he reflected, remembering how her eyes had devoured him when he had stood before her clad only in the breechclout as a Crow warrior.

Feeling suddenly restless, he scanned the dancers to see Patty still whirling and turning, enjoying a fast reel. He finished the drink and made his way from the compound to stroll along the all-but-deserted town street. The harvest moon hung low in the sky and looked somehow benevolent in its serene, perfect roundness. How many of those laughing and dancing inside the compound would see another harvest moon, he wondered. A nagging thought had come to stay with him ever since he'd questioned, listened, studied the Crow warrior's attacks. Was there more to Hawkwing's plans? It was not enough for a Crow warrior just to carry off women, even if it was purposely done to strike where the white men would hurt most. At the tribal fires during the long winter, when great coups were recounted and stories told, it was not enough to talk of capturing women. Not unless there was a greater reason. Fargo's eyes narrowed in thought as he strolled down the still street, the thought continuing to nag.

He'd reached the center of the silent town when the figures stepped from the shadows, two from behind a water trough, two from a darkened doorway. The dark-blue army uniforms with the yellow edging on the trousers caught the light of the full moon. The four figures halted, waiting, and Fargo took another step forward, scanned their faces, young but hard faces that had learned the ways of cruelty too early. The shortest of the four spoke, his voice cold, but Fargo had already guessed who they were. "We got something to settle with you, mister," the trooper said.

"Go back to the barracks. Don't make it worse for yourselves," Fargo said.

"Nobody's going to make a fool out of us," the soldier growled, and Fargo read the cold anger in their drawn, tight mouths but decided to try again.

"It wasn't meant that way. It was done to draw an object lesson for the colonel," Fargo said.

"We were docked a month's pay and drew thirty days' stable duty. We're going to take it out of your hide," the soldier insisted. "You don't play big shot on our backs."

Fargo's glance flicked over the quartet. They weren't wearing the standard army-issue sidearms. He drew a deep sigh as the four figures started toward him, two spreading out to move around the ends of the water trough. With the speed of a rattler's strike, Fargo's powerful arm shot out, seized the short trooper by the front of his uniform, and yanked him forward. The man's midsection hit the edge of the water trough, and Fargo heard the breath rush from him. Using his other hand, he slammed the man down into the water trough, held him underwater. The other three had halted in surprise for a moment, and Fargo kept the soldier at the bottom of the trough.

"Goddamn, git him," one of the others shouted as they shook themselves into action. Fargo released his grip on the man in the trough, turned, and ducked the rushing trio, dropping almost to the ground and bulling forward at the nearest pair of boots. He felt the man's legs go out from under him, and he dived forward under the toppling form. He rolled once, kicked out with one powerfully muscled leg. His foot smashed into the trooper's face as the man tried to regain his feet, and Fargo felt a nose break and heard the roar of pain as the figure fell backward. He rolled just in time to avoid a booted kick as the other two soldiers came at him. He got to one knee, twisted away again as the soldier tried another kick. As he twisted away, he lashed out, grasped the man's foot, and twisted. He was on his feet as the soldier sprawled face down on the ground. The fourth trooper came at him swinging, moving with the speed of youth. And the recklessness. Fargo's powerful arms blocked the first two wild blows; he ducked a third and lifted a short uppercut. It landed, sent the trooper staggering backward, glassy-eyed.

Out of the corner of his eye, Fargo saw the figure in the water trough, his head over the edge of the trough, throwing up a stream of water. The trooper in front of him shook off the blow and came at him again, and Fargo saw the other figure regaining his feet. He parried two more quick blows, feinted, and the younger man responded and ducked away, only to be caught with a short, driving blow to the jaw. He staggered backward, his legs rubbery. Fargo's arching left caught him on the other side of his jaw and lifted him from his feet, and the soldier flew backward to hit the ground and lie still. Fargo whirled as the fourth trooper rushed at him from the side, saw the dull gleam of the knife upraised in the man's hand. He twisted away, dropped almost to the ground as the knife whistled past his ear. "Goddamn sonofabitch," he heard the trooper curse through his teeth. Fargo managed to get part of his shoulder into the man's side, enough to knock him off balance as he went forward. As the soldier half stumbled to the side, Fargo brought a swinging left around, crashed his heavy fist into the man's side just under the last rib. He heard the soldier's harsh gasp, saw him double forward, turn, his face contorted with pain and fury. Fargo's piledriver left caught him alongside the jaw as he tried to bring the knife up again. The trooper half turned, fell sideways, landed on one knee, but still held onto the knife. Fargo brought a sledgehammer chopping blow down in a short arc. It smashed into the back of the man's neck, and the trooper fell forward with a rasped, breathy sound squeezed from his lips. He struck the ground face down, tried to raise his head, and fell back, unconscious.

Fargo took the knife from his limp hand. Standard army camping equipment. He grunted and flung it into the dark. He turned to survey the others. The soldier with the smashed nose lay on the ground, groaning softly, trying to halt the flow of claret from his face. Fargo glanced at the water trough to see the soldier had toppled out of the trough to the ground, still coughing up water. Fargo walked toward him, and the man started to pull himself to his feet, one hand clutching the side of the trough. He swung a wavering punch, almost fell, and Fargo seized him by one arm, spun him around, and flung him against the side of the trough, watched him slowly slide down to the ground.

Fargo stepped to the trooper just pulling himself to a sitting position, his jaw swollen out of shape. "That's twice you boys fucked it up. Don't try for three," Fargo said coldly. There was no answer from the misshapen jaw, but in the man's eyes he saw only the hatred of the defeated. He turned and walked from the scene as he found himself wondering if that had been the last of it. The knife attack disturbed him. It had changed an attempt at a brutal beating into an attempt to kill. He let himself hope they'd lick their wounds and common sense would take over, along with his warning.

He walked to the little rooming house, went to his room, and undressed to his shorts and stretched out on the bed. The lone window let him see out enough to enjoy the round moon as it slowly moved across the sky. He hadn't been there long when he heard the front door open and Patty's steps moving across the floor. She turned down the hallway, and he heard her come to a halt outside his door. He made a small wager with himself, and he smiled as the door slowly opened. Patty stepped into the room, her eyes finding his long, nearly naked figure as she pushed the door closed behind her, leaned back against it for a long, silent moment.

"Damn, Fargo, I've spent so long forgetting and you've brought it all back," she said.

"You never really forgot, Patty," he said. "We had

good times. There's no reason not to remember good times."

She moved from the door, lowered herself to the edge of the bed. Her hand reached out, came to rest on his shoulder, slowly moved down his bare skin to his chest, traced a path down across his powerful pectoral muscles, down to his hard, flat abdomen, moved down farther, onto his groin, down again, and her hand grew tight. He heard her gasped breath as she closed her fingers around him. Her body grew stiff and she arched her head backward, but her hand stayed around him, pressing tighter. "Oh . . . oh, God," she breathed, her eyes closed. Fargo reached up to her, unbuttoned the party blouse, slid it from her shoulders, pushed the top of her chemise down. Patty Rooney's breasts faced his eyes, slightly shallow at the tops, slightly long, yet filling out in lovely, rounded curves, a pale white in the dimness, the round circles darker, the nipples at the center of each circle pushing forward.

Fargo rose up almost to a sitting position, undid her skirt at the top, pushed it from her, and still she stayed with eyes closed, lips parted, her hand closed around the fullness of his organ, her fingers able to cover only a small part of its throbbing magnitude. Fargo's hand caressed her breasts, cupped the rounded undersides, and Patty shuddered in pleasure, a tiny smile coming to her parted lips. Her eyes half opened and she came forward, head bending low, her lips pushing her hand aside. "Oh, God, God, Fargo . . . oh, oh yes," she murmured and the gasped words became small sucking sounds and tiny cries of ecstasy. Patty Rooney pressed herself flat over his legs, her breasts soft against his thighs, and he let her have her pleasures, remembering, smiling as she began to move upward along his body, finally pulled her lips from him only to seek with other lips, softer, wetter, warmer. A moan

32

came from her as she sank down on him, her back arching as she began to move up and down in a rhythm that quickly grew stronger, faster. He flexed his pelvic muscles and began to move in rhythm with her.

"Oh, God . . . oh, oh, oh, aaaaaah . . ." Patty cried out, her cries growing stronger with each push. Suddenly her movements grew frenzied, a furious pumping. "Yes, yes . . . oh, yes, ah, ah . . . ah, God, I'm coming . . . I'm coming," he heard her cry out, and her arms clung to him, nails digging into his shoulders. Her hips tightened against him as she quivered atop him, her longish breasts shaking, her head thrown back, and only a soft gasping sound came from her now. The moment was little more than that, yet it stilled time and space until she fell forward over him, her long-waisted body limp. Finally she rolled over beside him, nuzzled lips to his ear. "Only you," she murmured.

"Only me what?" he questioned.

"Only you could make memories hold up," she said, and he felt her tongue caressing his face.

"I remember, too," Fargo said. "I remember that was only a beginning."

"Only a beginning." Patty smiled, turned onto her back, her arms reaching up to encircle his neck. He came over her and rested his body on her flat-hipped pelvis, felt her legs move at once, falling apart in instant welcome. Her tight rear rose with him, falling into immediate rhythm, and he smiled down at Patty's wide-mouthed, genial face. "As if we'd been doing it every night," he murmured, and she lifted to push against him, nodded happily, remembering, even as he did, how they had always fitted so comfortably. The night became theirs again, the world of passion and pleasure they created out of flesh and wanting, lust and loving, yesterday's memories and today's hungers.

Finally, Patty's long-waisted form lay beside him, thoroughly satiated, and, leaning upon one elbow, he enjoyed the loveliness of her slender, muscled body, a body where bony hips fitted perfectly, became part of its own kind of beauty. He ran his lips down the line of her stomach, and she murmured happily. He lay back, cradled her against him. She slept quickly, and he took longer, his thoughts suddenly full of restless musings. The round harvest moon was no longer visible through the window, and he found himself thinking of wagons rolling to lone homesteads with their trooper escorts dutifully riding herd. Fargo felt his mouth harden as he thought of the Crow warrior waiting. The Indian would strike, the opportunity too inviting to pass up, and only one thing stayed certain. The Indian would not do the expected. Fargo felt weariness press his eyes closed. Patty moved, snuggled closer, and he let sleep slide over him.

He slept soundly for the few hours before the day came to slip its way into the room. He woke, and at once the questions pushed themselves into his mind, defying, mocking. The night had brought no new insights, the facts still the same, the riddle unchanged. The Crow would take advantage of the hoedown, somehow, someway, but not the expected way and not during the night that had passed. Fargo's lips drew back in a half-grimace. That left only the new day, and Fargo's brow held a frown as he slid soundlessly from the bed, glanced at Patty's hard-asleep form. The new day, he repeated, but where in the new day, how in the new day? And most important, when? He pulled on clothes, his lips a thin line. Suddenly he halted, and the curse was a soft hiss that dropped from his lips. Dawn, he muttered silently. It had to be dawn. Sleep and the effects of the late-night revelry would still be clinging to the settlers. But that would lessen with every hour into the new day. Dawn, Fargo hissed. The unexpected time, the best time, the time when the effects of the night could still work for the Indian.

Fargo was running from the room as he strapped his gunbelt on. He raced from the house to the barn alongside and threw the saddle on the pinto. The morning sun was edging over the top of the hills. "Goddamn," he swore as he vaulted onto the pinto. Maybe he was too late already. He cursed and his eyes swept the land beyond the town, past the wooden tower of the fort, and he knew the bitter taste of helplessness. His mind raced through the list of the settlers he had come to know. The Isaacson family were the deepest into Crow country, their place alongside a heavy stand of timber that could easily hide the raiders. Of all the places, theirs was the most probable one. Fargo spurred the pinto into a full gallop, raced past the fort and the lone sentry standing on the lookout platform inside the closed gate. The sun was climbing into the sky, and Fargo cursed at it, wanted to hold it back, keep the dawn in place.

He rode hard, took a short cut across a rock-strewn ridge only the pinto could negotiate. He reached the Isaacson place and knew he'd guessed wrong as he saw Mrs. Isaacson carrying feed to the chickens. He waved at the woman's curious glance and raced on, cursing to himself. The Adcocks were a little more than a mile away, and he raced the horse hard until he came into sight of the stump-studded land and the small house. He saw Adcock come to the door of his house, a heavy musket in his hands. He lowered the gun as he recognized the rider, and Fargo saw his wife come to stand beside him. "Morning," the man called.

" 'Morning," Fargo answered, waved, and rode on, letting his mouth tighten when the Adcock place was out of sight. He made a wide circle from homestead to homestead as dawn became morning, and when he left the Ramsons', the sixth place on the outer perimeter, he had to wonder if he'd been mistaken about the Crow warrior's thinking. Had he struck one of the wagons last night? Fargo frowned and flung aside the thought. It refused to fit. He turned the pinto toward the second half-circle of settlers that had built back from the outer perimeter. His galloping visits revealed only quiet morning activities, and, swearing under his breath, he turned the pinto toward Sunwater as the morning sun burned full and warm.

He was riding the thick broomgrass of a gentle slope when he heard the sound, another horse, and he reined in, listened. No Crow, he grunted; the distinctive sound of shoed hooves pounded the ground. His eyes were on the top of the slope as the rider came into view, wheat hair gleaming in the sun, a pale-blue shirt that pulled tight across her breasts as they rose and fell in unison. Celia halted the brown gelding as she reached him, her eyes offering a kind of cool truce. "Good morning," she said.

"Shit it is. What the hell are you doing out here alone?" Fargo barked.

Her eyes darkened. "Simple good manners is more than you can manage, isn't it?" she snapped.

"Simple idiocy is more than I can take," he threw back. "Or are you just dying to see the inside of a Crow camp?"

"I hardly think there's any danger of that this morning," she said. "I was on my way to the Thompsons'."

"You hardly think," Fargo cut in and saw her lips tighten. She fastened him with a condescending stare.

"I do think you've a bad case of old-fashioned jealousy, Fargo," she said. "Here you are on this ridiculous mission and my uncle has things well in hand. I think the colonel is quite right about this Indian. It's obvious he knows the colonel is ready and waiting for him and he won't dare strike again." She allowed a smile of cold tolerance.

"You've plainly been out looking about. Have you seen any signs of him this morning?" she prodded.

Fargo's grim silence let her smile become more smug. "I'll see you to the Thompson place," he said.

"An apology for bad manners?" Celia asked.

"An attempt to save you from your own goddamn dumbness," he tossed back and sent the pinto into a fast trot.

She caught up with him in a moment, the smugness still wreathing her face. "Somehow, I thought you the kind of man who could admit being wrong," she commented.

"Somehow, I thought you the kind of girl who had a few brains," Fargo returned. "I guess we were both wrong." He tossed her a cold smile as her eyes flashed anger. "The colonel tell you it was all right for you to go riding out here alone?" he asked.

"No," she snapped. "He wasn't feeling well this morning. Martha told me he had a very bad headache. Uncle Henry's been bothered by terrible headaches the last few years."

Fargo was about to let out a snort of derision, but he held back, shot a sharp glance at Celia Wright, studied her for another moment and saw the touch of stiffness in her pretty face. "How long has the colonel been a hero to you?" he asked.

She gave a little shrug. "Ever since I was a little girl, I guess," she said. "He was always the exciting member of the family, leading an exciting life."

"See him often?" Fargo asked.

"Not often. At family reunions every few years. But I stayed in touch by letter. Visiting Uncle Henry was something I always wanted to do. Judy Thompson's invitation was the perfect excuse."

Fargo decided to say nothing more. Celia was not stupid. She'd have picked up signs even in her few days here, he was certain. But she was refusing to admit them, even to herself. Dreams die hard, and heroes that are hollow are a kind of betrayal. It'd hurt, he knew, and maybe she'd be able to keep looking away until she left. Maybe, he grunted silently. He spurred the pinto on around a cluster of alders, and she caught up to him again as he came in view of the Thompson place. He reined up and felt the fury stab into him, cast a glance at Celia. She had halted also, her lips parting, the surprise coming before the shock. "Goddamn," Fargo swore as he bolted forward, leaped from the saddle before the pinto came to a halt.

Jed Thompson lay on the ground, tied to a wagon wheel with his own lariat, his wife beside him. He was alive, his eyes trying to focus, Fargo saw, the one side of his face covered with blood where a tomahawk had hit him, the imprint of the flat side of the weapon still on his temple. Fargo dropped to one knee, began to untie the man. Celia's form came alongside him, her hands feverishly working on the woman's bonds. "Harriet, oh my God, Harriet," Celia murmured.

Harriet Thompson responded, her voice a hoarse sound. "Judy and little Ellie, they took them both," she said.

Inside Fargo, the fury seethed, exploded at the Crow and at himself. He hadn't been all wrong. He just hadn't been able to outguess the Crow, and he swore at himself for that. He expected the unexpected and yet he had guessed wrong. Not the families farthest out but the one closest in. *Goddamn,* he swore again silently. He hadn't underestimated the Indian. He simply hadn't given him enough credit. Hawkwing had matched cleverness with boldness, carrying through his way. Fargo rose, lifted Jed Thompson to his feet, and gave the man a kerchief to press to his face. He glanced at Celia, saw she was holding Harriet Thompson, and her eyes were still wide with horror. Jed Thompson's voice, a monotone, brought his attention back to the man.

"I opened the door to get some water from the well, same as I do every daybreak," the man intoned. "But I didn't check outside as I usually do. Guess I was still feeling the effects of last night."

"And they were there waiting," Fargo said. "The best time, the unexpected time." His glance stabbed at Celia.

The man nodded as he sank down to his knees. "My girls, both of them . . . oh, good God," he sobbed.

Fargo stared at Celia, his lake-blue eyes now blue flame, ignored the pain and shock in her face. "Still think the colonel was right?" he almost snarled. Her silence was made of loyalty shattered by the bitter reality in front of her. She tightened her grip on Harriet Thompson's arm.

"Tell Uncle Henry I'm staying here with Jed and Harriet," she said. She paused. "You are going back to Sunwater, aren't you?" she asked.

"In time," Fargo said. "I'll tell him, soon as his headache's better," he added grimly. He swung onto the pinto, gave Celia a hard glance, and she turned away. He rode forward, past the house and into the trees. Leaning to one side in the saddle, his eyes swept the ground. The Crow would have left in too much of a hurry to cover tracks, and it took him but a few minutes to pick up the broken pieces of bush, grass still flat from hooves coming down hard. Flat but not broken as a horseshoe would do with the edges. Unshod hooves of Indian ponies. He rode on, his eyes narrowed, counted three ponies. Hawkwing had brought only two braves with him, no large band that might attract attention but just enough to help with the captives. Fargo's mouth thinned in grudging admiration. He followed the tracks northward. They had ridden in single file, the hoofprints mingling together. Someone coming on the trail now could well think it but one horse and one rider. Fargo grunted again in appreciation of a clever woodsman.

The trail led upcountry, through heavy timber, out the other side, and down a lush, heavily brush-covered hill. Fargo halted, eyes narrowed, saw the trail disappear into the brush, and he turned his horse around, headed back the way he'd come. He'd gone far enough for now. To go on would be to risk riding into an ambush. He'd go on when he was ready, in his way and his time. Two could play that game.

3

Colonel Henry Kaster's hand trembled as he lifted the tall glass of gin and lemon juice to his lips, his reddened eyes marking the amount of booze he'd put away after he left the hoedown. Fargo's glance took in the other two people in the room. Martha was making pretensions of straightening up the small office, but her lips were drawn in tight, her back stiff with tension. A young lieutenant stood by, his uniform crisply pressed, his stance almost at attention, his face soft-cheeked and unlined, making him look not unlike a toy soldier.

"Goddamn redskinned bastard," the colonel blurted out in an explosion of words. "Stinkin' sonofabitch." He thrust the glass at Martha, and she took it, the square neckline of her calico dress dipping low enough to reveal the full swell of her more than ample breasts. The colonel glared at Fargo's icy stare. "So he made another raid. That doesn't make you right about anything," he accused.

"It doesn't make me exactly wrong," Fargo said with cold calm.

"If I hadn't had a party with each wagon last night he might have done a lot more," the colonel insisted.

"You keep missing the point, which is that he figured

41

you'd do that. He's not going to play it your way," Fargo said.

"He'll find out he's not dealing with some amateur. I'll send out two search patrols rightaway," the colonel said and turned to the young lieutenant. "Smith, you take one squad and have Clark take the other," he ordered.

Fargo didn't hide the contempt in his voice. "You've tried that. It won't work any better this time," he said and saw Lieutenant Smith's unlined face listening to him.

"Goddammit, lieutenant, don't waste time listening to this man. Get moving. I want those patrols out searching at once," the colonel snapped.

"Yes, sir," Lieutenant Smith said as he executed a smart turn and marched from the room.

The colonel's gaze returned to glare at the big, black-haired man in front of him. "If these patrols don't turn up anything I'll set a trap for him," he said.

"Hell will freeze over before you trap him," Fargo grunted.

"Then I'll hunt him down, goddammit," the colonel thundered. He reached out to take the glass Martha handed him and downed half of it in one long pull. Fargo watched the colorless eyes grow more watery, the reddened face growing redder in front of him.

"Back off. Leave him to me," he said.

The colonel frowned. "Not on your damn life, mister," the man threw back.

"You've an order telling you to do just that," Fargo said with icy calm.

The liquor fueled the man's angers. "Don't tell me about orders. I give the orders around here," he roared. "No goddamn general's going to tell me what to do in my command and no goddamn civilian's going to do my job."

"That Crow is up to something. I've got to find out what. If I can do that we might be able to save those women. Doesn't that mean anything to you?" Fargo returned.

"I'll save anybody that can be saved," the man answered, lulled on his drink.

Fargo leaned forward, flattening both palms on the desk, and his eyes were made of blue shale. "Now you hear me. I was sent to do a job and I'm going to do it. You'd better damn well stay out of my way," he said. He straightened, glanced at Martha Kaster, and saw the silent pleading in her dark-brown eyes.

The colonel drew himself straight, and Fargo was surprised to see how much malevolent hate could come into the watery eyes. "You're not going after him, not if I have to stop you myself," the man said. "That damn Crow is mine, and I'll show every last person I can bring him in. I'm in command here, mister, not you and not General Peterson, you hear me?"

Fargo turned away and strode from the room. He had said his piece. Even through his alcoholic haze the man had heard it. But Colonel Henry Kaster was full of the unpredictableness of the weak and the false courage of the bottle. How much did the Indian sense that? How much did his intuition, unclouded by man-made rules and manufactured behavior, tell him of the man who commanded the blue-clad troopers? Fargo made a grim noise inside himself. Perhaps too much, he pondered as he went past the sentry outside and swung onto the pinto.

He started toward the gate, slowed as he passed the four soldiers beside a hay wagon. One's face was still swollen out of shape, and two of the other three wore bandages as well as bruises. He saw the hatred gleam from their sullen eyes. "We're not finished with you," the one growled through his swollen face. Fargo rode past the four figures and wondered if it was little more than bluster and bravado now. They'd not forget his warning any more than they'd forget the beating.

He rode from the fort and steered the horse into town. At the water trough, he dismounted and let the pinto drink while he adjusted a cheek strap. He had just finished when he saw the couple coming toward him, the man short, stocky, a harsh face, the woman almost matching him in build. He pulled at memory and the name came to him. Donnato, Thomas and Rosa Donnato. The Crow had taken their daughter, Rosina, in a raid on their cabin near the edge of the perimeter.

"We want to talk to you, Fargo," Thomas Donnato said as he came to a halt, his brows lowered.

"Talk is you are going to go after the Indian soon," the woman said.

"That's right." Fargo nodded.

"He took Rosina over a month ago," the man remarked.

"I know," Fargo said. "I hope I can bring her back, if she's still alive. She and the others."

"No," the man blurted out.

Fargo felt his eyebrows lift. "No?"

"If she's still alive we don't want her back," the man growled.

Fargo felt the frown digging into his forehead. "What the hell are you saying?" he thrust.

"You heard him," the woman put in. "If she's alive you can leave her there."

Fargo felt the astonishment sweep through him as he stared at the woman, then at her husband. Their expressions were frozen, sullen anger in their faces. "For God's sake why?" he threw at them.

"She's no white woman anymore. She's a Crow. She's been a buck's woman," the man said.

"She's not our daughter anymore if she's still alive," Rosa Donnato said.

"For God's sake, she was captured, carried off. That sure as hell wasn't her fault," Fargo said, incredulousness still swirling through him.

"Staying alive is her fault," the man growled. "A girl with pride would have let them kill her, or she'd have killed herself before becoming a squaw woman."

"You're crazy, you know that?" Fargo shot back.

"You don't understand. A woman has to have pride. That's how it was in the old country. A girl with pride killed herself before she'd let them make her into a slut. Our daughter, Rosina, would do that. She'd kill herself before she let every buck use her."

"And if she didn't, you'll disown her," Fargo said, shaking his head in astonishment.

"She's not our daughter anymore if she's alive," the woman said, her face made of dark clay.

"Goddamn, if she's alive, I'm bringing her back, along with anyone else I can bring," Fargo said.

"No," the man exploded. "If she's alive you let her stay with the Crow."

"Maybe she'd be better off at that than with two such loving, understanding folks as you. Jesus, I think you're sick." Fargo spat.

"It is the old ways, the good ways," the man said.

"Screw your old ways. I'll bring back everyone I can," Fargo said.

"No, you won't. We're not having people look at us and say there go the Donnatos and their squaw daughter. You won't be ruining our good names and our lives with that," the man said.

"You hypocritical, twisted-up bastards. All you care about is yourselves and how people will think about you," Fargo said. "I'll do what I can for the girl, not for you."

He pulled himself onto the pinto, cast a last glance at the couple. Their short, chunky figures made them look not unlike a statue he'd once seen of two malignant, dwarflike evil spirits, a deep, dark foreboding in their brooding faces. He wheeled the pinto around and headed out of town. A terrible sourness coated his insides, and he felt as though he'd stepped into something dirty, a glimpse of a private sickness. He spurred the pinto into a fast trot, wanting the feel of clean, fresh air against his face. He'd gone a few dozen yards past the fort when he saw the rider coming toward him, wheat hair a yellow flash in the sun. She reined to a halt when she reached him.

"Back so soon?" Fargo asked.

"To pick up some clothes. I'm going to spend a few days with Jed and Harriet. They need someone around," Celia said, her round face solemn. Fargo made no comment, but a grimness came into his chiseled handsomeness. "You were right—is that what you want me to say?" Celia pushed at him.

"No. I wish I'd been wrong," Fargo told her.

Her light-brown eyes studied him. "You mean that, don't you?" she commented. "You're a strange man, Fargo. You carry your own set of rules in your own way."

"Why not?" Fargo said.

She drew a deep breath and the blue shirt grew smooth against her breasts. "What's going to happen to Judy and little Ellie?" she asked.

"Nothing good, you can be sure," Fargo said.

"Do you really think you can help them?"

"That depends."

"On whether you can get to Hawkwing's camp?"

"On what I find there," Fargo said. "That'll answer a lot of questions about what he's doing."

Celia frowned, her eyes searching Fargo's face. "But how can you, one man alone, do anything?" she pressed.

"I don't know," Fargo said. "Maybe I'll need help. If I do, will I get it?" He let the question find its own mark, his eyes waiting.

Celia responded to the sharp probe with instant protectiveness. "My uncle isn't that small. He wouldn't let personal feelings stand in the way of his duty," she said.

"Maybe it goes deeper than personal feelings," Fargo answered. "Anyway, I wasn't thinking of his sense of duty."

She frowned at the unstated in Fargo's voice. "I'm going to talk to him right now," she said.

"Better hurry. He's getting another one of his headaches," Fargo said.

Celia's lips tightened at the corners and she set herself for a moment, let her eyes soften. "Will you stop by at the Thompsons' before you set out after Hawkwing?" she asked.

"You want to kiss me goodbye?" Fargo asked.

Her chin lifted a fraction as she held his gaze. "If it'll help you get Judy and Ellie," she said.

He tossed her a grin. "Every little bit helps," he said.

"It'll also give the Thompsons added hope," Celia said and sent the gelding forward. Fargo watched her ride toward the fort, her back straight, her rear staying close to the saddle. She rode well, and he wondered if it was only horses as he turned the pinto and headed into the low hills.

He found a big red oak and settled down under its long, straight-hanging leaves. He let the afternoon drift away as he turned plans in his mind, plans that were as much hopes as they were anything else. The incident with Thomas and Rosa Donnato swam into his mind again, still disturbing, and he forced the sourness down. He'd seen the seamy, dark, sick side of human nature often enough so that he no longer tried to give it logic or explanation. Anyway, it was not the Donnatos that bothered him but Colonel Henry Kaster. Could he count on the man for anything?

Celia's words of personal dislike came to his mind, and he grunted in grimness. If only it were that simple. But Colonel Henry Kaster was not governed by personal dislike. He was a man corroded inside and out, hiding behind the uniform and the command, all of it but a facade of strength. It was a mask he had to keep up, for himself as much as for the world. That inner demon he could hide but not ignore, that core of weakness, would govern his decisions, not a sense of duty. That made the man so dangerous. The weak had to defend their masks, and they did so with a desperate need that distorted all else, right, wrong, reality, common sense, duty. For that mask, that disguise, was their only defense against the world, and the admission of their own failings. It was, in fact, a kind of strength turned inside out, but a strength that could only bring pain and anguish. Such was Colonel Henry Kaster, drink his private refuge from himself. When the chips were down, he could well be more concerned with his mask, his ambitions, than right. Or, Fargo mused, he could well be just too damn drunk to be good for anything.

Fargo pushed aside further speculation. The probabilities were all too negative, and he rose to his feet and swung onto the pinto. Two thin spirals of dust rose in the hill country, widely separated, and he watched their paths that marked the Colonel's patrols as they made wide circular sweeps of the countryside. Fargo's lips tightened in disgust, and he turned the pinto to head back to Sunwater as the dusk began to nibble its way across the land.

It was dark when he reached town and stabled the

pinto, climbed the few steps to the front door of the rooming house. He heard Patty in the kitchen but went directly to his room, undressed to shorts, washed, and lay across the bed, unable to shake the feeling of irritation, of valuable time being wasted. Delays, the unnecessary, stupid kind, always set him on edge, and he ignored the soft tinkling bell that announced dinner, his stomach too tightened for hunger. He managed to doze some, woke just as often, and it was midway into the evening when he heard the soft knock on the door.

"Come on in," he called and watched Patty enter. A loose gray, cotton nightdress took all shape and form away from her. "That's an awful outfit," he growled.

"It's for comfort, not for arousing base passions," she said. "You're in a dark mood." She waited, and he allowed a nod of agreement. "I heard about the Thompsons," Patty said. "Didn't expect you back."

"Didn't expect to be back," Fargo said, and Patty eased herself down on the edge of the bed, her eyes questioning. "Hell, I can't go now. The colonel's goddamn patrols will have everything stirred up good. Every Crow will be on the alert, watching," he rasped. "I've got to wait for them to settle down, dammit."

"How long?" Patty Rooney asked.

"I figure he'll send out another search sweep tomorrow and then call it off till he can think up something better," Fargo said, disgust heavy in his voice.

"That all that's bothering you?" Patty asked.

"That's enough. I don't like stupid delays," he snapped.

"I always say make the best of a bad bargain," Patty remarked, and Fargo saw her arms rise and lift, and the shapeless nightdress came off over her head in one swift motion. She dropped it on the floor and sat beautifully naked before him, her eyes almost defiant.

"Is that what you always say?" Fargo echoed.

She nodded and leaned forward, the twin long breasts dropping onto his chest. She pushed forward, brought them up to his lips. He opened his mouth for the soft, brownish nipples. "Why not?" he murmured as he let the warm softness fill his mouth. Patty made her words come true as she turned the clock back again, thoroughly and completely, until finally he slept with her long-waisted body wrapped around him.

The morning was full when he woke and watched Patty sit up and stretch, admired her thin loveliness, everything understated. She scooped up the nightdress and took it with her as she left, her narrow little rear wriggling itself out the door. Fargo lay back for a few moments, stretched his long frame out to its fullest, his body extending over the ends of the narrow bed. He rose and began to dress and felt the irritation descending upon him at once as he thought of another day of delay. Perhaps the colonel wouldn't send his patrols out searching again, Fargo mused, and knew it was a hollow hope. He smelled the beckoning aroma of fresh coffee from the kitchen just as he finished dressing. Patty had a clay mug of the black brew waiting for him. She had changed into a housedress and left the top unbuttoned, and he enjoyed the curve and dip of her breasts as she moved.

He rose when he finished the cup. "The coffee was good," he said.

"Just the coffee?" she returned, one eyebrow lifting.

"Everything was good." He laughed.

"Where are you going?" she asked.

"To ride some, watch some, think some," he said.

"You coming back?"

"Likely," Fargo said, and she nodded, a hint of satisfaction touching her face. He went to the barn and groomed the pinto enough to take off the road dust so that the jet-black fore and hindquarters glistened and the pure-white midsection gleamed. Finally he rode out of Sunwater and into the hill country. Once again he watched the colonel's troopers riding in the far distance, first one patrol, then another, making two wide circles just past the perimeter where the last of the settlers had cleared land. He watched the patrols ride in the clear, followed them as they disappeared into the heavy timber to finally emerge again, and he let his eyes, piercing as a hawk's gaze, peer far into the distance to catch the fleeting movement, a lone rider, then another far on the other side of a ridge. He half smiled with bitterness and quietly cursed the colonel and his useless patrols.

Finally he headed back to town, riding with unhurried casualness. He had little to do but wait now. When he reached the house he found Patty waiting just inside the doorway. She handed him the envelope, the U.S. Army official seal in one corner. "For you," she said. "Delivered by one of the colonel's troopers about a half hour ago."

Fargo opened the envelope with a frown of curiosity, his glance scanning the brief note penned on an army requisition form.

> Important we talk. Tonight, nine o'clock. My quarters.
>
> K.

Fargo's lips pursed in thought as he showed the note to Patty. She read it, handed it back with disdain touching her face. "Maybe he's having a sober moment," she commented.

"Maybe, but I don't go much with leopards changing spots," Fargo said.

"Maybe some do, when they get sober," Patty said, and Fargo half shrugged. "Soup is ready—turnip and beet with a little pork rind," Patty said.

"Sounds fine," Fargo said and pulled a chair to the table. Patty served the soup in large tin bowls, sat down opposite him, saying nothing as she spooned her soup. "You're very quiet tonight," he commented.

"I figure you'll be leaving come tomorrow," she said.

"If the damn patrols stop," he said. "But you knew that all along."

Her lips tightened. "Yes, I knew it and I still turned back the clock, and I'm sorry for doing it."

His glance was chiding. "You enjoyed it as much as I did, Patty," he said.

"You can enjoy something and be sorry for it," she snapped. She gathered up the soup bowls and put them in the sink. "I'll be going to bed early," she said, not looking at him. "Don't bother waking me."

"Whatever you say," he answered softly as she began to clean the dishes with pointed concentration. He went to his room and let the hours move on until it was time to go to the fort. He walked through the town, the night growing cooler even as he strode the short distance to where the fort rose in a black silhouette against the night sky. The sentry at the gate admitted him, and another young trooper saw him to the colonel's quarters. The window drapes were drawn, a thin sliver of lamplight edging the side of the curtains. The door opened at his knock, and Martha Kaster greeted him.

"Come in, please," she said. She closed the door behind him. She had her hair hanging loosely, and the lamplight turned low caught the planes of her face to make her seem twenty years younger. Only her body, filling a deep-red housedress with a low neckline, remained that of a ripe, mature woman, her full hips tightening the garment almost as much as the curve of her large breasts. The room, off the colonel's office, was simply furnished, a pine sideboard, a cushioned sofa and a corner cupboard. "Whiskey?" Martha Kaster asked.

"Why not?" Fargo said. She got a bottle from the sideboard and poured a shot glass of the liquid for him and one for herself. He watched her sip quickly from hers, take another sip, and draw in a deep sigh that pushed the fullness of her breasts up over the neckline of the dress in twin soft-cream mounds. He didn't hide his enjoyment of the moment and lifted his gaze to see her dark-brown eyes burning into him.

"The colonel's not here," Martha Kaster said, and Fargo let his eyebrows lift. "He left for Ellender this afternoon to see about a supply problem," she said.

"Then why did he send for me?" Fargo questioned.

"He didn't. I sent the note," Martha Kaster said. Fargo let the surprise in his face become a slow smile.

"Why'd you make it read as though it were from the colonel?" he slid at her. "No confidence in yourself?"

"I didn't want you to get the wrong idea," she said, too stiffly.

His smile grew broader. "You mean the right idea," he returned.

"I don't know what you mean," she tried.

"Hell you don't," Fargo snapped. "You've known since the first day I got here." He reached out, his hand closing around the back of her neck. He pulled her forward, kept hold of her, let his hand move along the soft hairs at the base of her neck, then down to the fleshier part of her neck, and pressed with a hard softness.

"No, don't," Martha said, and her voice was suddenly full of alarmed breathiness. "I want to talk about Henry," she murmured, but her eyes were dark with a different kind of wanting.

"Sure you do, but don't hang your bonnet on that,"

Fargo said. He moved his hand down on her back, felt her small gasp.

"I'd a reason for asking you to come, and it is about Henry," she protested.

"He's not a reason. He's an excuse," Fargo said harshly. He pulled her to him, pressed his lips onto her mouth. She murmured protest as her lips parted a fraction. He pressed harder. Her mouth came open a trifle more, enough for him to push his tongue in.

"No," she murmured as her hands tightened on his arms. "No, not yet." He pushed his tongue deeper, forcing her lips apart, a darting pink courier. His hand found the top of one large soft breast. "Oh, God," Martha Kaster breathed. Fargo's hand slipped inside the dress, moved across the soft mound, cupped its overflowing flesh, and the woman's head bent back, her hands dropping to her sides as she almost hung in his hands. A deep moaning rose from somewhere inside her. "Aaaaah . . . aaaaooooh . . . aaaah . . . aaah," the sound came, grew stronger, then fell away. Her eyes closed, Martha Kaster seemed transfixed. Fargo drew his hand from inside the top of her dress, stepped back. Slowly, Martha Kaster's head lifted, and her eyes came open to stare at him. The dim lamplight caught a few streaks of gray in her brown hair, made them seem silvery, lighted her face on the planes of her cheekbones, her nose and her forehead, danced on the high round rise of her breasts over the neckline of the dress. She stood before him with a majestic beauty that would have been contained and regal were it not for the burning wanting in her eyes.

"Still want to talk about Henry first?" Fargo asked softly.

Martha Kaster's hand lifted, unbuttoned a series of loops at the side of the dress, and Fargo watched the garment come loose, drop slowly from her to crumple on the floor at her feet. Her nakedness was commanding, full, a mature figure, yet not sagging, not loose, an echo of better days but firm in its fullness, large breasts with a whiteness that made the large brownish-pink areolas seem darker, the nipples large and protruding. His eyes followed the line of her abdomen to the convexity of her belly and below it, to a deep and dense, very curly, almost unruly, black thicket.

Martha Kaster moved backward slowly, silently, beckoning with her entire body, and he followed, glimpsed the large double bed in the adjoining room. He followed her, unbuckling gunbelt, taking off clothes, and he was naked when she sank back onto the big bed. Wordlessly, she spoke to him with her mouth parted, her eyes burning into him, and he found himself thinking how she resembled a person parched with thirst. He climbed onto the bed atop her and sank his face into the voluminous breasts, felt their capacious softness flow around him. His mouth found one large, brownish point, pulled on it.

"Aggghhh . . . aaaah . . . oh, oh, my God," Martha Kaster moaned from someplace deep inside her. As he rubbed his eager organ through the dense, unruly thicket the moan came again, louder this time, and he felt her thighs open, her legs lift. He didn't enter her, and she moaned again and now the moaning became a breathy call. "Please . . . oh, please . . . please . . . oh, Jesus, Fargo . . . Faaargoooo . . . oh, oh, oh God." He waited and felt her hands strike at his back as her belly came up, a soft, full mound, pushed against him. Martha Kaster quivered and moaned now and he dropped down from the unruly jet thicket and moved forward, into the soft portal quivering for him. "Ah . . . iiiiiii . . . iiieeee . . . oh, God, oh, oh," Martha Kaster gasped out, and Fargo felt her full-fleshed thighs close around him. She half-rolled, taking him with her and surprising him with her strength, rolled back again, and now she heaved and pushed with him, and her moans came again, deep, throbbing sounds, almost animal-like in character. She fell into a slow, deep rhythm that was both urgent yet with a holding back, and he came into unison with her. The rhythm became almost a rocking motion, quietly pleasurable, accompanied by Martha's deep moans.

He felt the rhythm telling on his organ, felt the urgent beginnings of that moment in space, and suddenly Martha Kaster pushed up hard against him, her full hips and belly beginning to jerk with tiny spasms, and the moans grew higher in pitch. He felt her thighs tighten around him, her hands clutch at his sides. "Ah, ah, ah, aaaah . . . iiieee . . . oh, God, Fargo, Fargo, my God, Fargo," she cried out, words approaching a scream. She was against him now, her pelvis locked against him, her body a series of fervid spasms, and suddenly she arched her back, rose, lifted him with her, stayed for what seemed an endless moment, and then the scream spiraled from her as she fell back on the bed. She seized his chest, pulled him to her face, muffled the scream against him as her pelvis pushed and pushed again in the spasmodic movements. He felt himself explode with her and her teeth were against his chest, pressing into his skin as she muffled her screams that rose higher and higher until they became an almost breathless, soundless hiss.

Finally she grew limp, quickly falling back from him, and he stayed inside her as she drew in deep drafts of air, her round belly trembling, her voluminous breasts rising and falling in gasping rhythm. It was perhaps five minutes before her eyes came to focus on him as he enjoyed the full-fleshed body that was hers. She saw the tiny smile touching his lips, the thoughts just behind his lake-blue eyes.

"Go on, what is it you're thinking?" she breathed.

56

"I'm thinking the colonel's not doing much of a job at keeping his woman satisfied," Fargo remarked.

He saw the bitterness come into her face. She rose up on one elbow, one large breast falling to the side. "The colonel hasn't been able to get it up for over two years," she said. Fargo's eyes questioned. "Too much booze," she said, and Fargo nodded. Too much booze could indeed do that.

"There's more than one way to satisfy a woman," Fargo commented.

The bitterness stayed in Martha Kaster's eyes. "If you're sober enough to do anything, or want to do anything," she answered.

"A waste," Fargo said.

"Of a good man?" she asked.

"Of a good woman," he answered.

Martha sat up and suddenly looked a little matronly. "Yes, a waste, and I won't have my whole life become a waste. That's why I must talk to you. You've got to let Henry get that damn Indian," she said. Fargo's expression stayed unchanging as he waited. "If he doesn't get that Indian he'll fall apart altogether."

"Seems to me he's done that already. The man's a lush. He shouldn't be in command of a damn flea circus," Fargo said coldly.

Martha Kaster's eyes darkened. Even stark naked she was able to wrap herself in a kind of dignity. "It'll get worse. He talks about suicide all the time. Your showing him up could push him into it. That's why you've got to let him go after that Indian. General Peterson doesn't understand the situation or he wouldn't have sent you."

"He understands the situation. That's exactly why he sent me. Frankly, I don't care if the colonel kills himself with a bottle or a bullet. His problems aren't my concern. I care about the lives of the settlers and all those poor

57

women that have been taken," Fargo said. "They come first in my book, not some incompetent, weak-kneed lush who's a disgrace to his uniform."

Martha's eyes held his. "You're a harsher man than I'd thought, Fargo."

"That's not harsh. That's plain truth. Hell, you'd be better off without him," Fargo told her.

"No!" Martha bit the word out as her eyes grew small. "Do you know what I'd get if Henry killed himself, one way or another? A quarter of his paycheck, that's what. That's what the army pays as a widow's pension. I've put too many years into Henry Kaster for that, too dammed many. Another five years of Henry drawing his full colonel's pay and I'll have enough put away to take care of myself, but that's not now. Right now Henry's my meal ticket. I want him alive, drawing his full pay for another five years."

"You're all heart, Martha," Fargo remarked. He saw her arm come up as she tried to slap him, and he caught her wrist.

"Don't talk to me about heart, goddammit," she spit at him. "He hasn't given a damn about me in years. All I'm good for is to clean and fill his glass. He doesn't feel, fondle, or fuck me, but by God he's going to feed and clothe me. He's not ducking out on that, too," she said. "Yes, I'm thinking of myself and no apologies for it."

Fargo watched her, and another question passed through his mind but he decided there was no need to press her further. He let her wrist go, and her hand dropped to her side. He felt almost sympathy for her. The road from bitterness to selfishness was a short one. Martha Kaster had taken it fully. She leaned forward, pressed him flat on the bed, lifted herself and pushed her breasts into his face. "Let Henry handle it, Fargo. Stay here in Sunwater and have me, whenever you want. I'll find the time and the place. Forget the damn Indian," she said, her voice growing husky. She rubbed her breasts across his face until he took one, then another, let each fill his mouth as Martha began to moan again, a deep, groaning sound, a kind of rapturous growl. She rolled, taking him with her, the dark, dense thicket rubbing against him as she lifted her torso to press upward. He felt himself grow eager at once, his tumescent organ probing, seeking, touching. "Oh, God . . . aaaah," Martha Kaster moaned as he let the tip rest against the soft-lipped, dark portal.

She pushed forward and upward to draw him in, and the room grew full with the sounds of her pleasure until, finally, she lay heaving and satiated beside him and he watched her full, rounded form slowly return to earth. It was not her starved hungers alone, Fargo decided. Martha Kaster was a woman of deep sexual drive. Her eyes opened to focus on him as he sat up, swung from the bed. "I'd best be going. Soldiers gossip like old wives," he said.

Martha sat up, her eyes watching him as he pulled on clothes, a tiny frown coming to her forehead as she studied him. "You're not going to stop, are you?" she said reflectively. "You're going after the Indian. This didn't make any difference."

"Don't take it personally," Fargo said. "You made a damn good try."

Martha Kaster's eyes continued to study him as he put on his gunbelt. "I misjudged you, Fargo. I didn't take you for the knight in shining armor kind. I thought you a more practical man."

"You were right," Fargo told her cheerfully.

Her frown deepened. "Then why are you going on with this?" she asked.

"Dammed if I know." He grinned at her as he started for the door.

"Fargo . . . don't do it," she called after him, in her

59

voice a note that seemed almost warning but he decided was desperation. He didn't look back, closed the door behind him and strode outside to cross the dark and still compound. He thought he saw a shadow move beside one of the barracks, duck behind a corner, but the dark was too deep for him to be certain. The sentry at the closed gate let him out through a small door at the side, and he moved down the deserted town street.

Martha Kaster lingered in his thoughts as he walked toward Patty's house. Her passion had been real, almost overwhelming, certainly made of hungers too long dormant. Yet that wasn't what he found himself thinking about. Her total bitterness stayed with him, overshadowing everything else. She was a woman imprisoned by her own set of desperations. Her half-truths, self-turned pleas, all were coming out of the same dark wellspring. Nothing mattered to Martha Kaster any longer but herself. She blamed it on her husband, and he sure as hell deserved most of the blame. But total, consuming selfishness was always partly a choice. You could fight against total bitterness or embrace it, and Martha Kaster had clutched it to herself with a vengeance that was disturbing.

Fargo felt the deep sigh escape him as he reached the rooming house. Martha Kaster would have to live with her bitterness, perhaps shrivel with it, a counterpart to her husband's corroding weakness.

He turned off thoughts of the woman and slipped into the house, made his way through the darkness to his room and undressed quickly, fell across the bed and slept until the morning was full. There was no need to hurry. He wanted to allow time for the Crow to settle down. When he rose and finished dressing, he went looking for Patty and found only a note and a hide pouch of dried beef with it on the kitchen table. "Good luck," he said, reading

60

the note aloud, and a wry smile passed across his lips. Patty had found reason to leave the house for the morning. Looking away was Patty's way of facing the unpleasant.

He went to the barn and saddled the pinto, finally rode from Sunwater in the bright, late-morning sun. His eyes scanned the ground a little way beyond the fort. There'd been no more patrols sent out, he saw in satisfaction. The fresh marks of a cavalry troop would have been still clear in the soil. He turned the pinto and headed for the Thompson place, drew near to it as the sun held at midday. He saw Jed Thompson working on a log fence, his body hanging heavy with despondency. The man halted, looked up with hollowed eyes as Fargo rode up and slid from the saddle.

"You setting out after them?" the man said, hope swimming into his eyes. Fargo nodded as Harriet Thompson came out of the house to stand beside her husband, her hand clasping his.

"Find my girls. Bring them back," the woman said, her face gaunt, her eyes red with sleeplessness.

Jed Thompson's face grew taut. "Just find that stinkin' Crow and I'll get my girls back," he said, his fists tightening.

"I'll do my best," Fargo said as the flash of wheat-blond hair appeared from behind the house, a basket of wash in her hands. Celia put the basket down and hurried to him as Jed and Harriet Thompson went into the house. Fargo's eyes met her searching gaze. "You said to stop by," he reminded her.

"Thank you," she answered. "I know it means a lot to Jed and Harriet to see you actually going out after Judy and Ellie."

"You see the colonel the other day?" Fargo asked almost casually.

Her face stiffened. "Yes," she said.

"Nothing else to say?" Fargo asked.

"Nothing," she snapped, and he didn't press further, satisfied that she'd seen for herself. Awareness, not admission, was all he wanted.

"I seem to remember another reason for my stopping by," he remarked.

"Yes," she said, her light-brown eyes narrowing a trifle. "For good luck."

"As I said, everything helps," he answered, and she stepped closer, lifted her face. He leaned foward and kissed her. Her lips were soft, her kiss sweet clover, almost a little girl's kiss. He pressed a little harder, felt her lips give a little, a hint of womanliness coming into the kiss, but only a hint as she pulled away. He recalled how her eyes had devoured his body when he'd stood before her as a Crow warrior, eyes that in no way echoed the little-girl sweetness of her kiss. She was made of parts that hadn't come together yet, he decided.

"I've a more practical way to help," Celia said. "I'm going with you."

The instant frown pulled the big man's brows together. "Hell you are," he bit out.

"I want to help get Judy and Ellie," she said.

"Then you keep your little ass right here," Fargo said, his voice growing crisp.

"Why?" she snapped back.

"Because I've a chance alone and I sure wouldn't take along some wet-nosed greenhorn," he speared.

She glowered at him, her lower lip pushing forward. "I could help," she said.

"You could help get my hide tattooed with Crow arrows," Fargo threw back. She continued to glower at him as he turned and climbed onto the pinto. He let a hard

62

smile touch his lips. "Thanks for the send-off. I hope I'll be back for another sample," he said.

"There won't be another sample," she said truculently.

"You can't say that," Fargo remarked.

"Why not?" she frowned.

"You might get to know yourself." He laughed and wheeled the pinto away. Her glower told him he had stabbed into tender places. Celia Wright was becoming aware of many things on this visit, he decided. She hadn't moved, her eyes watching him sullenly as he started to canter away. The Thompsons came to the doorway, and he waved at them, rode on into the trees. He followed the path he'd taken trailing the Crow raiding party but a few short mornings back, hurrying until he reached the hill heavy with low brush where he'd halted and turned back. This time he went into the thick, low brush, bending over in the saddle. Much of the brush had snapped back into place again, but there was enough trampled down to follow, and he trailed the Indian pony tracks through the hillside, upward into high forest country, reining up at a stream that suddenly appeared through the trees.

His eyes scanned the ground. They had paused here, let the horses drink, hoofprints clear in the soft bank of the stream. They had turned and followed the stream, he saw, riding back from the bank, but an occasional hoofprint landed in the soft soil, enough for him to track. He reined up again as he saw the pony marks turn abruptly, vanish in the water of the stream. He swept the other bank of the little stream with a long glance, spotted the hoofprints where the ponies had emerged.

He crossed the stream, cast an unhappy glance at the sky. The afternoon was growing short, and he returned his eyes to the ground. The stream had wandered, but now he saw the Crow had headed north again. But the heavy timberland was dry, the ground swallowing up prints. The tracks quickly became almost invisible, and he found himself moving very slowly, pausing frequently. He trailed not from tracks, now, but by other signs, tiny pieces of broken twigs, torn bits of shrub ends, maiden-hair fern pressed into the ground deeply enough to show that a heavy animal had done so. He worked against the growing dark and knew it was a losing battle. The trail took intense concentration, and when he heard the sound it first filtered through his consciousness. He halted, listened, and heard the hissing roar of a waterfall.

The trail followed the sound of the waterfall and then veered off. They had circled to pass the waterfall, now a loud, sibilant roar. It was almost dark, and Fargo broke off tracking and headed for the waterfall. He felt the cool, spray-laden air against his face as he neared it, pushed his way through thick foliage to come out on a rocky ledge facing a magnificent, tall waterfall cascading down a sheer expanse of rock, sending up sprays of wet mist where it landed in a rock pool. In the last light of the day he peered beyond the falls to see the rushing rapids of foaming white water fed by the cascading torrent, the racing water leaping and swirling over jagged rocks. He rode the pinto to the lee side of the falls, out of the spray, and dismounted. It was a good place to camp for the night, protected, cool, plenty of fresh water, set well back. He undressed quickly, put out his bedroll, and, naked, he washed at the edge of the falls, the spray a cool shower that took away the heat and dust of the day. Darkness was complete when he finished drying himself, put on shorts, and ate some of Patty's dried beef. He lay down, the roar of the falls a soothing sound that brought sleep quickly.

The early dawn came to mingle its faint light with the spray of the waterfall, painting the spot a soft gray. Fargo woke, sat up, and stretched, the roar of the falls surrounding him at once. He dressed, rose, strapped on his gunbelt as the grayness grew lighter, a hint of yellow in it as the sun slid down the rocks. He took a moment to watch the angry, racing white water of the rapids on the other side of the falls and then lowered himself onto his stomach, stretched out flat, and bent his head down to drink from one of the back pools. The cold, clear water was a bracing taste, and he had just started to lift his head when the shot exploded. It sounded like a cannon as it reverberated from the tall rocks.

The bullet slammed into the stone inches from his head to send up a spray of rock dust. Fargo tried to roll aside, but the bullet ricocheted with speed too fast for the eye to see. He felt the sharp, searing pain just over his right eye as it hit, and he fell on his side. Instantly, a black curtain came over his eyes. He shook his head, rose to one knee, but the black curtain stayed. "Damn," he muttered. He could move arms and legs, turn, roll, but he couldn't see. The ricochet had struck an optic nerve. He swore again. The falls had been everything he'd expected except for one thing, and he cursed at himself for the miscalculation. He hadn't thought about the roar of the falls drowning out all other sounds, allowing attackers to slip close enough for accurate shooting.

He stayed in a crouch, squeezed his eyes closed tight, opened them quickly. Only total blackness confronted him, and he listened, wondered if the Crow had rifles. He stayed low, let his ears pick up the sound of footsteps clambering along the rocks toward him. He drew his gun, grimaced as he strained his ears. He counted footsteps, two sets, decided there was perhaps a third, maybe a fourth. He couldn't be sure. He waited in his crouch till they neared him and then brought up the gun, fired in the direction of the sound. He heard shouts and curses, the sound of bodies diving to the side. No Crow, he knew now. Using ears instead of eyes, he heard the sound of footsteps running toward him from his right side. He spun on one knee, fired, knew his shots had missed. Confirmation came in the blow that landed against the side of his neck. He felt himself toppling sideways, and a kick sent the Colt spinning from his hand.

Fargo rolled, came up on his feet, half crouched, his ears straining. Footsteps were coming directly at him. He waited a moment longer in his sightless world and then, powerful legs driving him forward like a stallion, he charged, arms striking out ahead of him. He felt one blow smash into a face, heard the gasp of pain. In satisfaction, he felt another blow connect with skin and bone for another cry of pain.

"Sonofabitch," he heard a voice curse as he ducked, instinct guiding him, the blow brushing across the top of his head. He threw a left and it connected with ribs and he heard the sharp grunt. "Goddamn," another voice said. Fargo felt the blow crash down on his head, and he stumbled forward to land on one knee, shook his head, and his world remained totally black. Sight had left him entirely, and again he swore in bitterness. He dove forward, felt his arms wrap around a leg. Using all his strength, he twisted, and the leg bent.

"Owoooo . . . Jesus," the voice cried. Fargo felt the man go down hard, and fell half on top of him, missing with a sightless blow. The man still screamed in pain and Fargo half rose to drive his knee down, but a tremendous blow caught him atop the head, the sharp pain of it unmistakably from a gun butt. Fargo blinked, hoped the pain might somehow bring his vision back. But the blackness stayed and another blow struck hard. This one smashed the strength from him, and he felt himself collapsing. He tried to get up, but his arms had turned to rubber, his legs suddenly useless appendages. He lay prone, sightless, not completely unconscious yet unable to move, adrift in a strange, dark world. Voices filtered through his half-world.

"Sonofabitch."

"What do we do with him?"

"Put six slugs into him."

"No, it'll look better if he had an accident."

The voices faded, drifted away, and consciousness grew fainter. Fargo's fighting will struggled, demanded, and the voices drifted back again. "He's a heavy bastard," one came through the fog that surrounded him. Vaguely, Fargo was aware that he was being carried, yet he could do nothing, neither see nor move nor curse. But they were carrying him, the mind somehow relayed, and then all sensation faded again. The utter, total voice of complete nothingness engulfed him, that hanging place between life and death.

He felt nothing, knew nothing, as he was thrown wide and high into the churning waters of the rapids. As he hit the water, a flicker of consciousness came alive for the briefest of moments and he felt the wetness. But the instant vanished and he fell into unconsciousness again, unaware of how the water seized his body with glee, flinging it on, lifting and rolling it along its churning, rushing path. Nor could he know that, somehow, his shirt filled with air, became a small bladder that ballooned out to keep him afloat, acting as a makeshift life preserver as he was carried along the churning whitewater path.

But the raging water, carrying him downstream quickly, slammed him against a rock, and his body knew the pain though he felt nothing. The blow forced the air from his ballooned shirt, and he was sent tumbling head over heels through the rapids. The makeshift life preserver that had kept him from drowning vanished, and the water picked him up and lifted him on a rolling surge of power to send him crashing into a space between two rocks. His body became wedged into the space, his head just out of the water, and he hung there as the rapids swirled and raced past him. Unfeeling, unknowing, unconscious, his battered, bruised body lay wedged between the rocks. His attackers had long since left, and only the distant roar of the waterfall and the hissing of the racing rapids broke the silence. Death was close.

4

Pain. He felt pain and then the surging rush of relief. Only the alive felt pain. He lay absolutely still, and yet the pain persisted. His body seemed on fire with it. He let himself accommodate to the pain and remembering began its slow process, as though the mind were reluctant to relive the recent past. But he forced himself to remember, grimaced in pain as a muscle twitched. Slowly, it began to reassemble itself. The shot, first, totally unexpected, the ricochet of the bullet and then the blindness.

He grimaced again. His eyes were still closed, and he realized he feared opening them, let his thoughts return to the moment at the waterfall. After the bullet and the blindness there was the attack, his trying to fight back out of a sightless world. But there'd been another, last piece of subconscious awareness. It pushed itself up into his mind now. Wetness, the wetness of water, and then everything had fallen back into the void of nothingness, as though death had taken him. But he wasn't dead, Fargo told himself silently, gratefully. Slowly, he forced his eyes open, aware of the apprehension that coursed through him. Light filtered through to him, a blurred, amorphous haze of light at first. He closed his eyes and opened them again. The light remained and began to grow less hazy, brightness suffusing itself into the cloud in front of his eyes. The brightness stayed and took on darker places. Objects slowly began to come into focus.

Fargo felt the breath draw out of him, a sense of relief that far outdid the stab of pain in his chest. He could see again, he murmured in silent gratefulness. The objects took on contrast, shape. Leaves came into focus above him, then branches and pieces of sky. He started to pull himself up and gasped aloud in pain, fell back down at once, his entire body throbbing, ribs, back, arms, thighs. He lay still for a moment, then managed to turn his head slowly. He lay in a glen, deep-green foliage nearby. Fighting away the waves of pain, he raised his head enough to look down the length of his body and saw he was naked, large areas of black-and-blue bruise spots covering much of his body. A faint odor of some kind of oil drifted to his nostrils. He heard a sound, footsteps, turned his head. Wheat-blond hair swam into his line of vision.

"What in hell," Fargo murmured as he lay his head back on the ground. For a moment he wondered if he was dreaming, but the sharp stab of pain dismissed the thought. "What in hell," he murmured again.

"More or less what I said," he heard her answer and watched the wheat-blond hair come closer as Celia knelt down beside him.

"What you said when?" he muttered.

"When I found you," she answered.

He half-turned his head, ignoring the pain it caused to look at her. She was watching him, her eyes serious, almost grave. "Tell me about it," he said.

"I don't know all that much," she replied.

"Got to be more than I do. How come you found me?" he asked.

She slid from her knees to her rear, rested on the ground beside him. "I was angry enough to follow you," she began, her face growing into a half-pout. "I lost the trail by nightfall," she said. "I camped and wandered about some more when morning came. That's when I saw the men trying to catch an Ovaro. I recognized the horse at once and stayed back and watched. They couldn't get near him, and they finally gave up and rode off. I waited in the trees and followed the Ovaro when he started back. He criss-crossed through the timber, but I kept following him. He stopped at the waterfall, then moved along the bank of the rapids. That's when I spotted you."

"They must have tossed me in to drown," Fargo murmured.

"Somehow, the rapids wedged you between two rocks with your head out of the water. You were close enough to shore for me to bring you in with a lariat," Celia said.

Fargo tried to keep her in focus, but he saw her face growing fuzzy as the weakness started to slip over him again. Just the effort of concentrating had been exhausting. "How long . . . been here?" he managed to gasp out.

"Two days," Celia said as his eyes started to close. "Sleep. It's the best thing for you," he heard her say from far away, and he slept at once, unable to do anything but comply, unaware that Celia stretched out beside him on the cool grass.

The day was nearing an end when he woke. He felt better inside, but muscle and tissue still cried out in pain. Celia, awake, looked down at him, managing to look severe and enticing at the same time, a sizable feat, he thought.

"I owe you," he said.

"Yes," she answered crisply. "The water would have dislodged you sooner or later and you'd have gone under."

He found himself able to nod without searing pain and managed to push himself onto one elbow. She had put a

71

shirt over his groin, he saw and smiled inwardly. "The men you saw—how many were there?" he asked.

"Four," she answered.

Thoughts pulled at him. "They wear uniforms?" he asked and saw her frown.

"Uniforms?" she questioned. "No, they wore ordinary cowhand outfits."

Fargo lapsed into silent thought, lay back, and heard Celia at her saddlebag. She came toward him moments later with a narrow corked bottle, and when she opened it he smelled the slightly sweet odor of oil again. She dropped to her knees beside him. "Been rubbing you down with this. Cajeput oil, camomile, and olive oil. My grandmother's recipe for bruises and sprains. It works miracles," she said. "You should've seen what you looked like. The rapids all but broke you in half."

She began to rub the liniment over him, starting with his shoulders, down over his chest, into his ribcage. Her hands were gently strong, soothing, and he felt her kneading and massaging his bruises. She was good, he commented silently as he watched her. Her face bore a hint of sensual enjoyment and her hands moved down across his hard, flat abdomen, making little circular motions. He saw her lips part as her hands moved lower, down to his groin area, down to his thighs. She looked up suddenly, focused her eyes on a point in space as her hands massaged the liniment into him.

"Did you look away when I was unconscious?" he asked and watched the faint touch of pink appear in her cheeks.

"Of course," she said, but the words all but caught in her throat. Fargo smiled again, and the tiredness began to slip over him once more. Celia's soothing touch hastened the sleep that descended on him until he woke, hours later. He felt the warmth at once, saw that Celia had made a small fire close beside him. He pushed himself onto one elbow, saw the shirt draped across his groin again. He still hurt, but the fire had left his body and he could move without gasping out. Celia turned as he sat up, her eyes grave. She reached behind her, handed the big Colt .45 to him. "Found it beside the waterfall," she said.

"Thanks," Fargo said and remembered the gun being kicked from his hand. Gratefully, he put it atop his gunbelt curled near his head. A good gun became part of a man. You knew what you could count on, the speed of its trigger action, whether it bucked high or pulled to the right. "I owe you again," he said to Celia. He pulled himself up a little straighter. "It's been three days now," he said questioningly, and she nodded.

"It'll be four or five before you're able to travel," she said.

Fargo grimaced. "Plenty of time for Hawkwing to have struck again," he said.

Celia heated some beef jerky over the fire, and Fargo watched the way the tiny flame played across her face, catching the roundness of her cheeks, deepening shadows, giving her an ethereal quality. The firelight flickered across the white shirt she wore to curve around the undersides of her breasts and make them seem fuller. She handed him some of the beef jerky, and without the overwhelming pain he could enjoy eating. As he ate, he let his thoughts find voice. "No ordinary bushwhackers out for stealing," he said as if to himself.

"The men who jumped you?" Celia echoed.

"That's right. They were out to stop me from going on," Fargo said.

Celia gathered a frown on her forehead. "That's a terrible thing to say," she protested.

"It's true," Fargo said.

Celia's frown deepened. "Who would stop you from trying to save all those poor women?" she pushed at him.

"People that care more about themselves than they do anyone or anything else," Fargo told her.

He met Celia's eyes as anger crept into them. "You're thinking of the Colonel, aren't you?" she accused.

Fargo nodded. "He's at the top of the list. But there are others."

"Others?" she echoed, disbelief flooding her face. "No, I can't believe that of anyone, and certainly not Uncle Henry, no matter what you think of him."

Fargo pulled himself up straighter and his eyes fastened Celia with a hard stare. "You can't believe that of anyone," he repeated with harsh mockery. "How touching. You want to go over each, one by one? Or do you feel better staying Miss Innocence?" he challenged.

Her chin lifted. "All right, go on. I'll listen. I'm not afraid."

Fargo's intense handsomeness grew hard as shale. "Then we'll start with the good Colonel Henry Kaster," he said. "He's an incompetent, a damn fool, a drunk, and a weakling. Put that all together and it spells dangerous. All he has is a hollow mask. He'll do anything to protect that, to keep me from showing him up for what he is. That's all that counts with him. He'll sacrifice anyone or anything. In fact, he threatened to stop me. He could easily have hired four gunslingers."

Fargo paused, waited, but Celia's lips stayed turned down onto each other, offering neither defense nor admission. Fargo shifted on his elbow, felt the pain in his muscles at once. "Those four soldier boys," he went on. "They're a mean, sullen lot. They were willing to kill me once during a fight. All their threats since then might have been a lot more than hollow talk. It would be easy for them to switch into ordinary clothes, easy and safer.

And they'd have known I was going. Word travels fast around the compound. Their kind wouldn't care about anything except their revenge."

Celia's eyes were growing darker with horror and pain. "Go on," she said with effort.

"Then there is Martha, the loving wife," Fargo said, not hiding the sarcasm in his voice.

Celia's eyes almost exploded they grew so wide. "Martha? You can't be serious," she said.

Fargo's face held its grimness. "Serious as all hell," he tossed back. "Martha offered me everything she had to offer if I'd back away." Celia's stare was made of shock. "Martha's looking out for Martha. She's afraid if I show the colonel up for what he is he'll go off the deep end and she'll be left with nothing but a measly widow's pension. She'll do anything to keep the colonel drawing his full pay for another five years."

"You're making assumptions," Celia said.

"Hell I am. She spelled it all out for me, even showed me how grateful she could be," Fargo half smiled as Celia blinked in shock. "The colonel's not a husband to her any longer. He's an investment and she means to protect it. She knows that if I'd back off he could go on parading around and going through all his hollow motions and keep drawing that full pay."

"My God, oh, my God," Celia breathed. The shock stayed on her face as though it had been imprinted there.

"Then there are the Donnatos, Rosina's parents, a warm, loving pair," Fargo said with bitter anger. As Celia listened, he told her of his meeting with the man and woman that had soured his stomach. "They told me they'd never have me bring their idea of disgrace on them. They live by a code from another world that I think is sick and twisted. But it's everything to them, more than family, love, reason. Honor, their idea of honor, is all

75

they goddamn care about. They could have set those four after me and been proud of themselves."

Celia buried her face in her hands. "It's all so terrible, all of it. I can't believe it, I can't," she said, words muffled.

"You don't want to believe it," Fargo corrected. "But it's all true. One of them was behind it. I figure I'll find out in time, if I'm still around to find out." Fargo lay back and carefully stretched his body. The pain came at once, but it was bearable, his muscles regaining their suppleness. "I'll ride tomorrow," he said. "I've got to. There's been too much time lost now."

Celia took her face from her hands to gaze at him. "Better get some more sleep, then," she said. He nodded, let his body relax, and felt the tiredness quickly move through him. He turned on his side, watched Celia as she stared into the dying fire. It'd be a while before she slept, he knew. Illusions hurt when they shatter, almost as much as idols that turn into dust. He closed his eyes and slept at once, let the restorative powers of deep slumber work through the night.

The sun on his face, a warm, gentle touch, woke him, and he pushed himself up onto one elbow, flexed muscles, satisfied that he could stand the pain. He saw Celia sit up. A thin blue nightdress half off one side revealed a lovely rounded shoulder and the soft swell of a tanned breast. She was still rubbing sleep from her eyes as he pulled on shorts and rose to his feet, wincing once or twice. She got her eyes open, looked up at him, her eyes moving across his body.

"We'll go back to the waterfall. I've got to go back there to pick up the trail again, and I want to wash this oil off," he told her.

She rose, took her clothes in hand. "Turn around," she said.

"Why? It's my turn to look," he said with a grin.

She threw an annoyed glance back at him as she strode toward the trees. Her rear moved deliciously under the filmy nightdress. Events, reality, were waking her to the harsh side of human nature, a shattering of innocence. Was she just as innocent in other areas? If so, it was time for another kind of awakening, an awakening to pleasures that could balance out the awakening in pain. He finished dressing with the thought hanging in his mind, and Celia returned, pushing her hands through the wheat hair, white shirt open at the neck, tanned mounds filling the space provocatively. Only her troubled eyes were a jarring note in her fresh, unspoiled loveliness.

He mounted the pinto with less pain than he'd expected and led the way back to the falls, grimaced as the roar of the water reached his ears. Lessons learned the hard way were the kind remembered. At the edge of the rushing rapids, where the bank lessened the swift flow of the current, he undressed to immerse himself in the cool water, washing away the traces of oil still on his skin. He came out to see Celia, on her horse, looking the other way, and he smiled to himself as he dried with a towel from his saddlebag. When he finished, dressed once more, she returned her eyes to him.

"I'll be going with you," she said.

"We've been through that," Fargo answered.

"That was before," she said tartly. "You owe me, remember? Or was that all so much talk?"

Fargo's face was stony. "You know better," he said.

"Then it's settled," she returned. "Besides, I'd never find my way back alone, and you can't spare the time to take me back." Her eyes held a lofty smugness.

He allowed a wry smile. She was tossing fact and indebtedness at him in a two-pronged assault that was as

77

unanswerable as it was unvarnished. "You learn fast," he conceded.

"Always," she said.

His face grew hard again. "It could be your last trip anywhere."

She thought for another moment. "Going back alone could be my last trip, too," she said, and he had to nod agreement. "Besides, I want to do anything I can to help save Judy and the others," she added.

Fargo studied her, decided to keep the words inside himself for the moment, and he turned the pinto north. With Celia staying close behind, he returned to where the tracks had veered off to circle the falls. The trail, more than four days old now, proved dammed hard to pick up. Once again he found himself putting together stray signs and random marks, a hoofprint here, another there, a long path of rosy-capped amanitas lying trampled in a line leading into the woodland. He had halted at one point, his lips drawn back as he searched for a sign, and Celia came alongside.

"They seemed to head north. Why not just go that way?" she suggested.

"Never go by what it seems," he growled. "You guess only when there's nothing left but that."

"Such as now, I'd say," she commented.

"I wouldn't," he snapped, his eyes opening wider as he spotted a place in the trees ahead and spurred the pinto to it. Celia came up quickly, her eyes scanning a half-dozen small branches broken off at the ends between two large red cedars. "They went through here," Fargo said, indicating the split edges of the snapped branches.

"How do you know? Maybe deer broke them off," Celia questioned.

"Deer move too carefully to snap off this many branches. Elk or moose might do it, but then they'd have snapped branches higher up, too. These are the shoulder height of an Indian pony," Fargo said and moved forward between the two cedars into the woodland. He managed to pick up enough signs to keep on the trail, leaves torn from low branches as riders pushed their way through, a half-circle where the Crow had halted for some reason. The woodland finally thinned out to become low hill country, slopes and timber stands. Fargo pressed on faster, and halfway up a long slope he reined the pinto in sharply. Celia, halted beside him, started to speak when his hand reached out to cover her mouth. She blinked and he drew his hand back, pointed to the top of the slope. Beyond it, from someplace on the other side, a thin line of smoke drifted upward.

Fargo dismounted, and Celia followed his example, stood beside him as his eyes swept the hills to the right. He started up, moving into tree cover, leading the pinto behind him. "This is as far as we go for now," he told her as they moved upward in the trees. She frowned, and he pointed to a cave opening in a flat side of rock amid the trees. He tethered the horses outside, ducked his head as he went into the dark opening to return in a moment. "It'll do," he said. "We hole up inside until we can get closer and stay alive."

"By night?" she said.

"More or less," he answered, securing the horses under a dense cover of cedars.

Celia had stepped halfway into the cave. "It's dank in here. And it smells," she said.

"Get a small fire going inside," Fargo told her. "That'll take the dampness and the mustiness out."

He searched nearby, found a rock large enough to cover most of the entranceway, and pushed it into place. It left just enough room for him to squeeze through and would allow the smoke to dissipate into the air. As Celia got the fire started, he brought saddle blankets into the cave, rolled them open, and sank down on one. The wince escaped his lips as he stretched out, his body protesting against the long hours in the saddle.

"You should have rested another day," Celia said.

"No time for it," Fargo answered, grimacing as he flexed his muscles. "Got any more of that oil?" he asked.

She nodded, rose, and slipped through the narrow opening at the mouth of the cave to go to her saddlebag. He was undressed when she returned, the small fire just large enough to dry out the cave with its warmth. Purposely, he'd lain his shorts over his groin, and he saw her quick glance as she returned, the narrow bottle in her hand. She knelt down beside his all but naked form and her hands pressed onto his chest with the oil, spreading it slowly, her face staying composed but her tongue flicking across her lips. She rubbed slowly, her touch soothing, sensuous, and she couldn't keep the tactile pleasure of skin on skin from her eyes. The little fire half behind her turned the wheat-blond hair into shafts of gold. Her body moved with supple grace as she massaged his chest, her breasts inside the blouse pressing first one side of the material, then the other in a softly undulating rhythm.

Fargo felt himself growing hard, desire translating itself into flesh and blood, refusing denial. Her hands pressed, massaged down across his abdomen, touched the skin of his groin. He heard her breathe in soft half-gasps, her eyes fixed on the beauty of his body, her fingers caressing as much as massaging. She'd just begun to draw her hands away when the shorts across his groin were flung aside, almost angrily, by the erect, swollen, eager member, thrusting upward in pulsating invitation. He heard Celia's sharp intake of breath as he grasped her wrist, pulled her hand forward onto the warm, moist soft hardness.

"Oh! Oh . . . aaaah . . . ah, my God," she gasped. "No, no . . . oh, no." But he kept her hand there, felt her fingers opening and closing, trying to draw back yet curling around him, opening again, closing again. "No, oh, please . . . no," Celia gasped, desire and denial in her breath.

He released her wrist in a sudden movement. Her hand stayed around his throbbing maleness for another moment and then, with a gasped cry, she pulled it back. But Fargo was twisting her around, bringing his mouth onto her lips. She pushed against him, but her lips opened and he tasted the sweet clover of her kiss again, felt her lips try to stay firm, proper, then part wider. He pushed his tongue forward, quick, almost harsh little movements. "No," Celia breathed even as her mouth opened wider for him. He found her tongue, pressed against it with his own and felt her respond, moving forward to touch his mouth, reach deeper.

His hand pushed down over one tanned breast, the shirt falling open. "No, oh, please . . . oh no, oh . . . oh, God," Celia gasped as she pulled away, fell back, both breasts thrusting up at him, both beautifully rounded, nipples tanned, too, a brown-pink, small matching circles around each. He caressed each with his hands, moving his fingers along the soft undersides, tracing a slow line around each brown-pink tip. Celia's body twitched, tiny little spasms, and she continued to make protesting noises with her lips as her hands crept along his chest. He glanced up at her eyes. The light-brown orbs were staring at him, a transfixed stare, as though she were caught in some halfway world. He leaned down and drew one breast into his mouth, pulling gently, letting his tongue press onto the little tip.

"Ah . . . ah . . . ooooooh, oh, God, oh yes, oh, oh . . . oh, God," Celia cried out, each word rising higher than the other. He pushed against her skirt with one hand, felt it fall away, pushed undergarments free to see her legs, well formed, held together, rise up to almost touch her stomach, hiding her pubic area. He pressed both hands over her breasts, his thumbs rubbing the tips that had found a tiny erectness of their own. Her hand made fluttering motions along his abdomen, and he took it, put her fingers around his throbbing maleness. "Aaaaiiiiii . . ." she cried out, and her legs straightened, stayed down to reveal a neat little dark triangle at the bottom of a deliciously rounded little belly. He moved his hand down to it, and now Celia was gasping out sounds as her legs twitched, moved apart, came together, the wanting and the resisting all still a tumult inside her.

His hand pushed between her thighs, and she closed her legs around it at once. He paused, felt her relaxed, moved against the edge of the dark, wet, waiting lips. Celia cried out in a breath-filled gasp, and suddenly the tumult vanished. Her torso pushed forward against him, her thighs falling open. "Yes, oh, God yes . . . oh, oh please, yes," she breathed. Her hand clutched at him, found him, and she shuddered in pleasure. She turned for him, all desire now, wanting and hunger entwined. He came atop her, moved the top of his organ against her, and she screamed into his chest. He pushed slowly, found her tightness, knew the meaning, pushed again slowly. The tiny gasp of pain was drowned out by her cry of wanting. He moved into her, cried out himself in pleasure at the warm tightness of her. She twitched again, and he felt the little round belly pressed up against his hard-muscled body, its own little mound of sensuousness. Her triangle mingled with his own and he moved with excruciatingly sensuous slowness inside her. Her hands dug into his back as she fell into rhythm with him. The coupling dance grew in intensity, and he pressed his mouth over her breasts.

"Fargo—oh, my God, Fargo," she gasped, and he let her move to her own pace as he felt her begin to tremble under him. "Oh . . . oh . . . aaaaaiiiiii . . ." she cried out as the trembling seized her. Her body rose under him, pushed forward, and now she was crying and calling, asking and urging, and he felt the contractions around his organ before she realized what was happening. He thrust hard as suddenly she trembled as though she were a wire suddenly pulled taut. "Yes, yes . . . oh, my God, my God . . . yes . . . now, now, now," she half screamed as the world exploded for her. He let himself go with her, and she was sobbing, half screaming into his chest.

When she fell back onto the blanket, he saw the almost wild stare in her eyes, eyes that looked at him as though they were someplace else. He reached gently down, caressed each little brown-pink nipple with his tongue until he felt her body relax, and when he met her eyes again they were only soft with satisfaction. The night had fallen, he noticed. The cave was almost black, the fire but a few burning embers. He rose, put a few small sticks on the fire, and it flamed up at once. She held her arms out for him as he came down beside her again.

"I'd say you were quite better," she remarked.

"I'd say I'll be needing another massage pretty soon," he answered.

"You're no doubt right," Celia agreed happily. She rose on one elbow, both breasts falling beautifully to one side, her face suddenly clouded. "Have we time?" she asked.

"Plenty of time," he told her.

"Good," she murmured, lying back, and he enjoyed the beauty of her tiny-tipped breasts, the shallowness of her abdomen and the delicious little mound of her belly. She watched his eyes moving across her body, pausing at the neat, black triangle. "What are you thinking?" she asked.

"Wondering," he corrected. "About how you can be so blond on top and so dark below."

"I've wondered about that myself," she said. She rolled over to press herself against his chest. "I didn't come wanting this," she said. He made no reply, and she sat up, peered at him, her brow furrowing. A wry smile came to her lips. " 'You might even get to know yourself,' " she quoted.

"Was I wrong?" Fargo asked, pulling her down to him.

"No," she breathed. "But I want to know myself more."

"There's time," he said, and his mouth found her breast. There was more than enough time, and Celia's awakening reached higher the second time until finally she lay beside him, satiated and murmuring small, happy sounds. She slept for a spell, and he joined her, felt her wake, rise to add a few more pieces of wood to the fire. He watched as she sat, knees drawn up under her chin, her face grave as she stared into the waking flames.

"Serious thoughts?" he asked.

"I was thinking about Judy," Celia said.

"You can't do it, you know," Fargo remarked.

Her glance at him was quick. "Can't do what?"

"Make up for other people's failings," he said.

"I don't know what you're talking about," she said too stiffly.

"Hell you don't," Fargo snapped. "That's why you followed me. You want to help Judy and the others because the colonel failed them, because they wouldn't be Crow captives if he were the man and officer he ought to be."

She frowned back, peered at his strong, intense handsomeness. "How did you know?" she said quietly.

"People leave trails. Some are outside, some are inside,

84

but they're not all that different. They all leave signs, marks, imprints. You just have to know where to look and how to look," he told her.

Celia's mouth formed a half-smile, a tinge of admiration in it. "The Trailsman," she murmured, and settled herself against him and slept again. He catnapped with her, kissed her awake a half hour before the dawn.

"Get dressed," he said as he pulled from her arms and quickly began to draw on clothes. He went outside to the horses, had just finished tying the stirrups up to the saddle as she came outside, and she helped as he took the bits from the horses' mouths and tied the rein chains with the reins. Satisfied there was no metal or rattle or scrape, he swung onto the pinto. "Let's go," he said, and watched Celia start to turn after him, her face grave, the wheat-blond hair a dim silver in the new dawn's half-light.

He led the way down the hillside and up the other slope, moving the pinto with slow and deliberate steps. When he neared the crest of the slope he slid from the Ovaro, waited as Celia followed. Tying the horses to a low brush, he went into a crouch, started up the rest of the slope. He dropped to his stomach as he reached the crest, watched to be certain Celia did the same, motioned for her to lie flat beside him. She crawled forward as his gaze moved down the other side of the slope. The new day began to give definition to the land below. The Crow camp lay at the bottom of the slope. Fargo spied two braves, guards more than sentries, one at each end of the camp. Two tipis, he saw, felt the furrow touch his brow as his eyes carefully moved across the rest of the camp.

As he watched, the camp began to wake, a thin brave stepping from the nearest tipi, two more following. He felt Celia's hand tighten on his arm as, from the other tipi, two old squaws emerged, each leading a line of captive women, strung together by ropes tied to their ankles and a second rope around their necks. The ankle ropes gave them room enough to walk, the neck ropes were tighter. Fargo's eyes swept along the two rows of captive women. They were somewhat torn and tattered, but all still in their clothes, and again he felt the crease furrow his brow. Celia's fingers dug deeper into his arm.

"There's Judy," she whispered. "The third one with the dark-green dress. And that's Ellie behind her."

Fargo took in a tall girl, plain, mildly attractive, with long brown hair. The younger girl behind her shorter and plumper. He looked across the other row, paused at one young woman, black, long hair and black eyes, large breasts that almost hung out of a dress with the top buttons torn away, a sturdy, peasant quality to her. Rosina Donnato, he wagered silently. Four more old squaws, wrinkled, stooped crones, emerged from the tipi, each carrying a length of peeled sapling branch. They struck the captives across the buttocks and the backs of their legs, chattered and gestured, and the women began to pick up firewood at the edge of the camp. A dozen more Crow warriors emerged from the nearest tipi to stand in a half-circle as the captive women placed the wood on the small fire. Fargo watched as one reached his hands up the skirt of a young woman and laughed as she cried out, fell to her knees. But he pulled his hand back and one of the wrinkled old crones hit her viciously across the back. The Crow buck grew angry at once, pulled the sapling away from the old squaw and pushed her aside.

The young white woman rose to her feet and shuffled off with the others in a kind of lock-step. Fargo's frown stayed now as he watched the scene below, taking in every detail of the camp, taking note of everything that took place. He watched with narrowed eyes as the women were given food out of a large wooden bowl that one of the old

86

squaws passed among them. "What are they giving them?" Celia whispered.

"Corn gruel, I'd guess," Fargo said. "They often flavor it with honey." His eyes swept across the captives again. The women had one thing in common, eyes laced with despair and faces drawn with fear. He took his gaze from the captives as the braves stood, turned to the farthest tipi. A lone figure emerged, a single eagle's feather rising from his browband. He wore only a breechclout and leggings with beadwork designs. The other braves stepped back respectfully as the figure moved toward them, and Fargo felt Celia's hand on his arm grow tight.

"Hawkwing?" she breathed, and he nodded, watched as the Crow moved on legs tightly muscled. Not a big man, the Indian was lean and lithe as a mountain cat, every movement smooth, long muscles rippling in the sunlight, and Fargo knew the Crow could move with power, speed, and agility. He let his gaze linger on the Indian's face, a prominent nose, a cold, imperious face with small black eyes and hair that hung long and heavy with buffalo oil from the browband. The old squaws stepped back as the Crow chieftain moved up and down the two rows of captives as though he were a general reviewing troops. A woman who looked away had her head yanked up by the hair to face the small, sharp black eyes, and Fargo saw the cruelty held back in the Crow as the man twisted the woman's hair until she cried out. He released her with contempt, waited to make certain she didn't look away again, then moved on.

When he finished examining the captives he said something to one of the wrinkled old squaws and the women were marched back into the tipi. One of the old crones hit a slow-moving young girl, and Hawkwing reprimanded her instantly.

Fargo, his eyes narrowed, started to slide backward.

"I've seen enough. Let's go before some of those bucks come up here hunting rabbit for dinner," he said.

He slid backward on his stomach, Celia alongside him, until they reached the horses. He swung onto the pinto and began to move slowly down the slope. Celia's round cheeks were drawn with nervousness, he saw, and a faint line of perspiration ran across the smoothness of her upper lip. "Can't we go faster, a trot, at least?" she asked.

"No," he said. "You'd be surprised how far off an Indian can pick up sound and vibration. Keep at a walk." He saw Celia rein in, glance behind her. "Pay attention to your horse. Stay away from those branches on the ground," he said curtly. She swerved the bay to one side, her mouth a tight line. Not until they reached the tree cover and he turned up toward the cave in the woodland beyond did she relax. He heard the deep sigh come from her as they reached the cave and tethered the horses under heavy tree cover. Fargo slipped inside first, sat down in the dim light inside the little cave. She entered, slid down beside him, her face grave.

"What do we do now, wait for dark?" she asked.

"Wait for dark so we can get out of here," Fargo said.

Celia's frown was instant. "Aren't you going to do anything about Judy and the others?" she asked.

He shook his head. "Too many squaws with them, too many ropes. It'd take us too long to cut them free."

"Then we go back for help. We know where he has his camp, now," Celia said.

"Maybe," Fargo muttered, frowned into space.

"Maybe?" Celia flared. "What does that mean?"

"It means something's wrong about this camp, about all of it here," Fargo said.

"Why do you say that?"

"No kids, no young squaws, no cooking pits, no racks for drying meat and skins, only two tipis, not even a

88

travois anywhere," Fargo shot back. "All he has here are some young bucks and some old squaws. This isn't his real camp. This has been set up to hold the women he takes."

"Why?" Celia questioned.

Fargo shrugged. "I don't figure that yet," he said. "There's something else. He's treating his captives very carefully in terms of Crow captives. They're being fed, almost protected from the old squaws. They've been left with their clothes. Ordinarily, they'd be stripped naked, passed from buck to buck, and then turned over to the squaws as slaves. That's not happened to these women."

"Why not?" Celia frowned.

"He wants them alive and in recognizably good shape," Fargo said. "He's got a reason, damn him."

"We've still got to go back and get help. We owe it to those waiting to tell them their wives and daughters are still alive. That's the least we can do," Celia insisted.

Fargo's lips drew back in distaste. "I suppose so, but going back will mean trouble," he said.

"You mean with Uncle Henry?" she said.

"Who else?" he said curtly. "All he'll see is his perfect opportunity to play the big rescuer. He'll want to go charging in."

"And you don't agree with that," Celia said.

"Not yet," Fargo said.

"Uncle Henry may think differently. He may surprise you," Celia said.

"He'll surprise me when a rattlesnake gives milk," Fargo snapped. He saw the resentment flood into her face. "Loyalty dies hard," he commented.

"Dammit, there's such a thing as having confidence," she snapped back. "You know what I think? I think Hawkwing is holding his captives as hostages. I think he's afraid the colonel will trap him, and he wants the captives to bargain with. I think he's afraid of the colonel and his troops."

"You're half right. He's holding the women as some kind of hostage, but not for that reason," Fargo said. "He's as afraid of the colonel as a cougar is afraid of a groundhog. He's watched the colonel's moves. He knows very well what kind of a damn fool he is. In fact, I'd bet that he's counting on that fact. I just wish I knew how."

Celia retired into glum silence, and Fargo lay back, his lips still drawn tight with distaste. He'd have to go back, he pondered. There was no way they'd have time to cut the women free. The camp was too tightly knit, everything too close together. He was still pondering the options, wishing for ones that didn't exist, when Celia moved, lay down alongside him.

"I hope you're all wrong," she muttered into his chest.

"I hope so, too," he agreed solemnly.

Celia settled herself against him, saying nothing more, napped as the hours went by. His mind was too full of whirling thoughts, riddles that offered no answers. Only one thing had grown clear. As he'd suspected from the start, the Crow chieftain was not out simply to capture women. He prepared to have greater stories to tell around the winter campfires. Fargo catnapped, waited for time to pass. The morning had slipped into the afternoon, the little cave a dim, silent world, when he heard the sound from outside, the high, thin cry of a flight of cedar waxwings suddenly disturbed. He was on his feet at once, Celia waking, her eyes on him as he strode toward the entrance to the little cave.

He slipped through the slim opening and dropped to one knee as Celia came up behind him in time to hear his soft curse. His eyes were fixed halfway down the hill where two bucks on their ponies had halted, their heads raised, turning first one way then the other.

"What are they doing?" Celia whispered.

"Sniffing," Fargo said. "They've smelled the horses. The breeze is blowing in their direction, dammit." He felt his lips tighten as the two Crow continued to sniff the air, saw the one motion with his hand and start up the slope. "Sonofabitch," Fargo breathed. His hand around the butt of the big Colt drew away. He could easily pick them both off, but the shots would bring the others at once. He had to get them without noise, and his eyes watched as the two riders carefully moved up through the woods, one behind the other.

"Get your horse," he said to Celia. "Start down, let them see you. They'll go right after you. Turn and lead them past here."

Celia nodded, fought down the fear that had leaped into her eyes, he saw, and he moved away as she reached the bay and climbed into the saddle. He found a thick patch of low brush amid the red cedars as Celia started down the hill, sank down into it, and drew the double-edged throwing knife from the sheath on the calf of his leg, the thin, perfectly balanced weapon some people called an Arkansas toothpick. He watched, his arm drawn back, the handle of the knife resting in the palm of his hand. He had to cut the odds fifty percent in one silent instant. There'd be no second chance, he knew. He couldn't leave one to summon help while he fought the other. Celia flashed in front of his vision as she moved down the hill, and he saw the two Crow spot her. She did a good job, reined up short, as though she had seen them at the very same instant.

She wheeled the horse and started to race up through the wooded land, and Fargo saw the two Crow go into instant pursuit. The first Crow closed in on her. As she raced the bay past Fargo, his arm drew back and he paused, gauging distance, angle, the height of the Crow as the Indian pursued his quarry. The second Crow was close behind him, and Fargo made himself ignore him, brought his complete concentration on the first brave. He paused another instant and then the thin blade hurtled through the air, leaving his hand with a faint whirring sound. The Crow had just passed the brush where he waited and Fargo saw the blade enter the back of his neck, a small, perfectly thrown javelin that pierced the Indian's neck through, the tip of the blade coming out the other side.

The Crow's hands flew to his neck in futile, fluttering movements as he toppled backward from his pony. The second Crow reined up, frowned down at the writhing figure on the ground, unable to realize what had happened until he glimpsed the knifeblade through the man's throat. He uttered a sharp cry, spun in the saddle, the tomahawk instantly drawn from around his waist. His eyes widened as he saw the big, black-haired figure leaping from the brush at him. He sent the tomahawk downward in a short arc at his attacker. Fargo dived upward, twisted, prepared to take part of the tomahawk's blow. The force of it nonetheless sent a wave of pain through his shoulder and down along his arm. But he got his hands around the Indian's leg and yanked, pulling the figure from the pony's bare back. The buck landed on his side when he hit the ground, still clutching the tomahawk in one hand. He started to whirl, but Fargo's kick caught him alongside the head and he went backward.

Fargo swung his right arm to force the numbed pain from it, felt muscles respond, but the moment had given the Crow time to regain his feet. One side of his face bleeding from Fargo's kick, the Indian came in crouching, the tomahawk at the ready. Fargo thought of using the butt end of the Colt but discarded the idea. It would be a clumsy weapon that would hinder his movements more than help him. Speed and outmaneuvering the Crow was his only chance. The Indian came in, feinted with one hand, but Fargo refused to respond and the Crow feinted again. On his third try, Fargo lashed out with a left hook. He whirled and pulled his arm down as the Crow crossed the tomahawk in a sharp sideways blow. Fargo felt the edge of the ax scrape the side of his arm as he spun away.

The Indian was quicker than most, he saw. He circled to the right, stepped back, and saw Celia out of the corner of his eye. She had reined up, her eyes wide with fright as she looked on. The Crow moved forward, and Fargo's eyes moved from his hands to his feet and back again, watching for signs of his next moves. When he glimpsed the Indian's left foot dig into the ground he ducked away to the right just in time to avoid the arching swing of the short-handled ax. He tried a countering blow, a hard, fast uppercut. It missed as the Crow pulled back, and once again Fargo found himself spinning away from the tomahawk's blow.

He circled again, wondered how long he could avoid the Crow's lightning-fast strikes without having to use the big Colt. He tried feinting, saw the Indian duck away, and managed to cross a looping left that landed on the man's temple. The Crow stumbled to one side, and Fargo went after him, cursed as he had to leap and spin away as the Indian brought the tomahawk slicing the air in an upward arc. His right foot landed on a half-dozen loose leaves on the ground and he felt his leg go out from under him. He saw the Crow diving in at once, tomahawk raised. Fargo flung himself flat and the Indian half fell over him, stumbled, regained his footing, and whirled to bring the weapon down again. Celia's cry and the sound of the horse racing forward cut into the moment. The Crow whirled, ax raised, his body in a half-crouch, his eyes on Celia as she raced the bay at him. He lifted the tomahawk to throw it directly at her. Fargo's tackle hit him around the knees as he was about to let the ax fly and he went down. This time Fargo got a powerful left flush on the Crow's jaw, felt his body go soft. He brought a brutal overhand right smashing into the Indian's face and felt his nose crack open. A guttural sound came from the Crow as the tomahawk fell from his hand.

Fargo dived for the weapon, his hand closing around it. The Crow was starting to pull himself up when Fargo brought the ax down in a smashing blow. The sharp edge burst the man's forehead as though it were a melon, and Fargo ducked away from the shower of blood and bone. "My God," he heard Celia gasp and saw her bent over in the saddle, her face averted. He pushed the Crow's lifeless form aside and rose to his feet, felt the strained harshness of his own breath. He strode to the other buck and retrieved the double-edged throwing knife, cleaned it off on the grass, and walked to where the pinto waited.

Celia was still half bent over in the saddle when he returned. "Let's go," he said brusquely. "When they don't come back to the camp there'll be others come looking for them. I want to be far enough away by then."

She nodded, spurred the bay beside him. "Will they come after us?" she asked.

He thought for a moment. "Not likely. They'll spend time trying to figure who and how, but with no bullets or rifle-stock wounds, they won't figure it was a white. They'll likely blame a party of Sioux or Assiniboine."

He put the Ovaro into a canter, and Celia followed. They had reached the other side of the hills and were into the thick red cedars when the day began to slip away. He continued on, reached the waterfall, and circled around it when dark made it impossible to move farther through the woodlands. He halted, tethered the horses in the inky blackness, and spread his bedroll between two tree trunks.

"No sense is using two bedrolls," Celia said as he felt her come against him, warm, smooth, and entirely naked.

"No sense at all," he agreed as he found a down-soft breast against his lips. The stygian dark of the night and the deep forest became a kind of cocoon, shutting out all yesterdays and all tomorrows, a welcome world for more reasons than Celia's eager wanting. Not until her cries of ecstasy turned to soft murmurings of satisfaction did he sleep.

5

"I want to be there when you meet with him," Celia had insisted as they'd neared Sunwater.

"You think he'll be different with you there, or are you just curious?" Fargo had asked.

"A little of both, perhaps," she said.

Fargo had said no more, and the misgivings had continued to ride with him, invisible, unwelcome companions that prodded and poked with each passing hour. Now, as he faced Colonel Henry Kaster's reddened eyes and flushed countenance, he could almost hear their silent, mocking laughter. He glanced at Celia and saw the bitterness in her face as the last hopeful illusion shattered. His gaze paused on Martha in the background, her eyes showing apprehension more than surprise. But Martha was contained enough to keep emotions in rein.

"I thought I'd seen the last of you," the Colonel said, cutting into his thoughts.

"Any special reason?" Fargo pushed at him.

The man shrugged. "The Crow. I figured they'd done you in," he said.

"The Crow or somebody," Fargo commented.

"Or somebody," the man echoed, took a drink from the glass on the desk. Fargo's quick glance sought out

Celia, but she gave nothing back. "Dammit, Fargo, you'd no right to take my niece on your crazy wild-goose chase," the colonel suddenly roared, indulging in self-righteous anger.

Celia answered at once. "He didn't take me. I followed him," she said sternly. The colonel tossed her a disapproving glance.

"She did well," Fargo said.

"And how well did you do, Fargo?'" the man snapped. "Does your coming back mean anything?"

Fargo remained silent, second and third thoughts racing through his mind. Celia read the last-minute changes mirrored in the hard blue shale of his eyes. "Fargo found the camp," she blurted, cutting off his change of mind. "The women were all there, all alive."

Fargo shot her an angry glance she refused to meet. "Well, now, maybe you have come in handy," he heard the Colonel say. The man raised his voice, leaned back, and shouted an order. "Lieutenant Smith, come in here," he said, and Fargo watched the young-faced officer step in from the adjoining room. "Take a few troopers and spread the word that the captives are all alive," he said.

"Yes, sir," the young lieutenant said and hurried from the room. Fargo felt his anger spiraling as the colonel bestowed a tolerant smile on him.

"Now let's have the rest, Fargo. The camp, where is it?" he said.

"The rest is that there's something wrong. He's holding the women for a reason. He's planning something," Fargo said.

"Nonsense. You're trying to make him into something more than what he is, just a thieving coyote who's taken to capturing women because it's easier than capturing men," the man answered with infuriating smugness.

"He's planning something, goddammit," Fargo growled.

The colonel held on to his smugness. "I'll put an end to it, if so," he said. "Now where's that camp of his?"

"You go charging in there and you'll get every one of those women killed," Fargo said.

"You leave military tactics up to me, Fargo," the man bristled.

"You and that bunch of green kids you've got as soldiers. The blind leading the deaf. No thanks," Fargo bit out, watched the man's flushed face grow redder.

"You watch your damned tongue, mister," the colonel flared. "Proper field tactics will ensure the safety of the captives."

"Bullshit," Fargo snapped. "There's only one way to give them an even chance at staying alive. Find out why he's holding them, what he's planning, and then make your moves around it. But I'll need more time, time to go back, trail again, watch, listen, wait."

The colonel let a pompous smile come to his face. "I'm no fool. I know why you want to go back. You're looking for a way to bring Hawkwing in yourself. That'd impress General Peterson. He might hire you for something else."

Fargo heard Celia's voice cut in, anger in it. "That's not so, Uncle Henry. That's unfair," she said.

"This isn't your concern," the man said sharply, turning to her. "Perhaps he's fooled you, but I know his kind."

"All you know is a bottle," Fargo rasped.

"Dammit, where is that camp?" the colonel roared, slamming his fist on the desk. Martha caught the glass of gin and lemon juice as it almost toppled from the edge.

"Go find it yourself," Fargo said.

"Are you refusing to tell me?" the man roared, drawing on all his pompousness.

"Are you going to give me time?" Fargo returned.

"No, goddamn you," the man thundered, his face dark red.

"Then go fuck yourself, colonel, sir," Fargo said.

He watched the man draw in his breath, his mouth make little movements of fury. "I'll have you slapped into jail for withholding information important to the United States Army," he said.

"Go ahead. I can use a rest," Fargo said, his tone casual but his eyes peering hard into the man's colorless orbs. As he expected, for all his besotted bluster, Colonel Henry Kaster recognized a stand-off when he saw one. He waited as the man drew his alcoholic fury in.

"You've got till tomorrow morning to tell me where that camp is or you'll be behind bars," the colonel said stiffly.

"Try it the other way," Fargo said and saw the man's frown. "You've got till tomorrow morning to tell me I'll have the time I need."

"Get out," the man shouted.

"My pleasure," Fargo said. His eyes met Martha's as he turned, saw the wide, uncertain apprehension still in her eyes. He strode from the room, had reached the sunlight outside when he heard Celia's voice. He halted as she came up to him.

"Heard enough?" he asked bitterly.

"All right, you were right," she conceded. "But let me work on him tonight. I think I can get him to listen to reason. It's worth a try, Fargo."

"Try hard. Think about your friend Judy," he said coldly as he walked away from her, took the pinto, and started across the compound to the gate. His eyes searched the troopers and found three of the four he sought. Their eyes showed only sullen anger again, but then he hadn't expected more. It was too late for surprise. They'd heard of his arrival by now.

He left the compound, started to turn down into Sunwater, then he heard the clatter of wagons being driven hard, halted to see a half-dozen wagons racing toward him from outside the town. Some twenty people were crowded into the wagons, he guessed at a quick count. They came to a halt, half-surrounding him. He saw the Adcocks, the Isaacsons, the Ramsons, the Thompsons, and all the others he'd come to know by face more than by name. And on the edge of the crowd, the Donnatos, faces made of stone, eyes burning him with cold fire.

"We heard but we wanted to hear more, from you, Fargo," Herb Isaacson said. "They're all alive? Is it true?"

"Far as I could tell," Fargo said. "They're not having a picnic but they're in fair shape."

"Thank God, thank God," a woman's voice wailed.

"What's being done to rescue them?" a man called.

Fargo paused, thought about sending them to the colonel. But he'd only give them confidence he'd no right to give, assurances he'd no way of making good, and they deserved better than that. Honesty that wouldn't destroy hope yet not compromise itself. "The colonel has his plans. I have mine. We'll take the best," he said. "Too late won't do any good and too soon won't do any better." They took his words in with grave, unsmiling faces, fear still holding relief and hope in bondage. His eyes sought out the Donnatos. "I'll do my dammedest to bring them all back alive," he said. Their faces remained as stone.

"That's all we can ask," Ben Adcock said, and the others murmured agreement. Fargo watched some turn around to go back to their homes and others continue into town. He saw the Donnatos watch him ride on down Sunwater's single street until he was out of sight, as though they were trying to spear him with a silent curse or an evil hex. He halted at Patty's house, dismounted, and went inside to find her in the foyer, waiting.

"You rent my room out?" he asked, unsmiling.

"Not yet," she said, her eyes grave.

He reached out, pulled her to him. She came but threw no arms around him. She rested her head against his chest and nothing more. "Thanks for the dried beef and the note," he said. "You shouldn't have ducked out like that."

"I shouldn't have turned the clock back either," Patty said flatly. His big hand pressed against her thinness, half-encircled her slender waist, so different to the touch from Celia's rounded body. "News travels fast. I heard you found the women. Can you save them?" Patty asked, pulling back to search his face.

"I don't know. It might depend on that drunken incompetent in uniform," Fargo said.

"Why'd you take his niece along?" Patty asked, her tone suddenly edged.

"News does get around fast," Fargo commented.

"Hell, that got around last week when the colonel went looking for her," Patty said, and he saw the cattiness come into her eyes. "You told me you were going alone. I might have volunteered if you needed female companionship that badly," she said.

"Meow," he said. Patty's eyes stayed cool. "I didn't take her. She followed me. If truth be known, she saved my life," he said.

Patty took in his words, but the edge stayed with her. "I suppose you were properly grateful," she said. "Don't tell me. I don't want to know."

"I wasn't going to tell you," Fargo said. "You never were the bitchy type," he said thoughtfully.

"It's called caring. It's called not wanting to be part of a parade. It's remembering how you always were and

101

being sorry you turned back the clock," she said, and there was anger in her voice.

"Is it called wanting more than you can have?" he asked.

She looked away. "Maybe," she said softly.

He pressed his hand against her back again, a gentle touch. "I'm going to turn in. I can use the extra sleep," he said. He brushed her cheek with his lips as he passed and strode down the hallway to the room. He undressed quickly and lay down on the bed to fall asleep at once, weary muscles taking their own demands. He slept soundly and the night grew long, turned the corner of the midnight hour, when he woke, the faint sound catching his ears. His hand went to the big Colt at the side of his pillow, then he saw the slender form lying down on the bed beside him. He felt her warm nakedness, her narrow waist moving to fit against his hip.

"You said I never was the bitchy type," she murmured. "I'm just glad you're here and in one piece and I'm tired of wasted nights."

"Good enough," he said as Patty's hand crept down to the waking offertory between his legs, her fingers closing around its expanding potency. As was her pleasure, she began their lovemaking once again by moving her lips across his body, tracing a pathway of tiny fires to the altar of her worship.

"Oh . . . oh . . . aaah . . . oh, God," she murmured as she buried her face against him, cradling his throbbing organ against her cheek, caressing, admiring, letting all the years of wanting come forth in an ecstasy of touch and feel and taste. Later, as she brought her narrow, long-waisted body over his, he satisfied all her wantings, more than met her every desire, and knew once again that passion wore many faces, pleasure many bodies.

She had coffee made when he rose in the morning and

somehow managed to look very proper in a flowered housedress, as though the day had brought an entirely new person on the scene. "You sorry about last night?" he asked over the coffee cup's rim, more curious than concerned.

"No," she said briskly. "Nights with you are like rainbows. You never know when you'll see another, and I'm sorry about that." She rose, took away her coffee cup, allowing him no chance to say anything. It was just as well, he reflected, for he had nothing to say. She was right, and until another time came, a time when scores were settled and debts paid, he could do nothing else. He rose and she came into the room at once. "You'll be going today?" she asked.

"One way or the other," he said.

She came to lean against him. "Come back," she murmured.

"I'm not figuring anything else," he told her, patted her flat little rear, and hurried from the house. He was riding the pinto toward the fort when he saw the Donnatos loading their wagon with provisions at the general store. Their unyielding faces turned away from him as though he were the plague. He rode on, into the fort and into the compound. Two of the four troopers he had tangled with were on sentry duty, and he saw their eyes watch him ride in with undisguised hate. He dismounted at the colonel's quarters, and Martha was the first to greet him, blocking his path in the small outside entranceway.

"You've done enough. Let him do the rest, Fargo," she pleaded. "God, I'll make it up to you."

"Will you make it up to all those captive women if he gets them killed?" Fargo struck back harshly. She backed into the office ahead of him, her face set.

"I'll tell the colonel you're here," she said, and disappeared into the next room.

Colonel Kaster appeared a few moments after, his uniform jacket half-buttoned. The smell of gin mingled with the scent of shaving cream, but he seemed relatively sober as he eased himself into the chair behind the desk.

"I've thought the matter over," the colonel began. "You said if I backed off, gave you time to pursue your theories, you'd tell me where Hawkwing has his captives."

"More or less," Fargo said and felt distinctly uneasy.

"I've decided to go along with you. I'll hold back while you find out whatever else you can," the colonel said, making the pronouncement sound benevolent, and Fargo swore again as he kept the surprise from his face. He had expected something else, another round of bluff and bluster, perhaps an attempt to see how far he could be pushed. The man's sudden reasonableness was more than a little out of character, and he felt the uneasiness inside him growing. He studied the colonel's face, but the weakness in it was its own kind of mask, the watery, colorless eyes revealing nothing. "Celia has convinced me you are efficient and sincere in your concern for the captives," the colonel said with infuriating gratuitousness. "Now I'll expect you to keep your end of the agreement," the man said. "Where's that camp?"

Fargo swore silently again. He'd made the offer of exchange to buy the time he needed and now was sorry he'd done so. Yet he'd no choice but to live with it. His uneasiness was perhaps simply surprise at the man's about-face. Maybe he was underestimating the power of a few hours of sobriety, an excursion into clear thinking instead of an alcoholic haze. Colonel Kaster could have seen the light of rational thinking.

"The camp, Fargo, where is it?" he heard the man say.

"I was figuring on telling you when I get back," Fargo tried and saw the colonel's brows lift.

"What if you don't get back, Fargo? I'd be left with

nothing, then," he said. Fargo swore silently. Logic on top of cooperation and reasonableness. The colonel was showing what a dose of sobriety could do. "I've kept my end of the bargain. I'm giving you the time you want. I expect you to keep your end, or isn't your word that important?" the colonel pushed at him.

Fargo released his breath in a deep sigh. "In the mountain country due north," he said, putting away all his misgivings.

"Directions, Fargo," the colonel snapped, and Fargo proceeded to draw him a verbal map, marking each natural guidepost, giving him full instructions on trails and shortcuts. "How long will it take me to reach the camp?" the colonel questioned.

Fargo thought for a moment. "Moving with a full troop, I'd guess three days, maybe four," he said.

Colonel Kaster rose, and his lips formed something close to a sneer. "You have your time, Fargo. Make the most of it. I'll see you when you get back," he said.

Fargo nodded and left the office. He found himself hoping the colonel could hold on to his relative sobriety. It didn't make him any more competent or any more likable, but it did make him possible to deal with, at least. He mounted the pinto, glimpsed Martha at a window watching him as he rode from the compound. He gave a harsh grunt. She, the Donnatos, the four troopers, and the good colonel himself, they all watched and followed him with their eyes. Which of them silently cursed a failed attempt at stopping him? He wondered as he rode from the fort and headed north. He'd not gone far when he saw the horse waiting alongside the road and with it the wheat hair flashing in the noon sun. Wearing a pale-blue shirt, Celia looked radiantly fresh. He drew to a halt beside her.

"You did well," he said. "Thanks."

"It took a lot of arguing, and then he suddenly

agreed," she said. "Just when I was beginning to think he wouldn't listen to me at all."

"Seems he did," Fargo said.

Her eyes were wide and serious. "What are you going to do?"

"Look for a proper camp someplace," he said. "I'm betting it's not too far from where he's holding the women. Maybe the answers will be there." His mouth grew tight, and he let sternness come into his eyes. "I'm going alone," he said.

"I think I earned my way last time," Celia answered coolly.

"You did," he agreed. "But I'm still going alone. It's best that way."

Her half-smile was rueful. "Don't worry, you won't have to look over your shoulder. I won't be following you this time. I promised the colonel I'd stay put. He insisted on that before he agreed to give you more time." She leaned from the saddle suddenly and lifted her lips to his, her mouth opening quickly, her tongue a quick, eager messenger. "But I'll be waiting," she said, pulling away. "Come back safely."

He nodded, hearing the echo of Patty's words inside himself. He'd have to be as careful when he returned as when he trailed the Crow, he told himself as he rode away. He turned from the road a dozen yards on and let the pinto take his time moving up a steep slope where the bristlegrass grew thick. He was familiar with the way now, with no need to painfully search for trails. The dark came and he continued till he was beyond the waterfall, the sound of it no longer reaching his ears. He camped then in a small hollow of pale-barked cottonwoods. He wanted the pinto to have a good night's rest. The horse had done more than enough traveling during the past days, and a tired horse was no help at the unexpected moments. There'd be more than enough of those, he was certain.

He made a small fire, mostly of brush and leaves, just enough to take the chill off the night, and lay down on his bedroll in the silence of the woods. The sound of deer caught his ears, soft, delicate steps as they filtered their way ghostlike through the trees. He heard scurrying, short, fast steps, a marten or a weasel. He closed his eyes and slept, and the dark had turned the midnight hour when his eyes snapped open as the sound reached his ears. He lay still, listening, his hand stealing to the Colt at his side. A horse and rider, moving in a zigzag pattern, he grunted. He raised himself onto his elbows, moved back from the almost burned-out fire, the Colt in his hand. The horseman was making no effort at being stealthy, the mount brushing hard against branches, moving noisily through brush, coming nearer. Suddenly the rider halted, then moved forward, a straight line toward the flickering fire.

Fargo brought the Colt up, his eyes narrowed on the darkness of the trees, waited, and then the dark shape appeared, moving toward the embers on the ground. The horse moved into the clear of the little hollow, and Fargo sat up straighter, his jaw dropping open as he peered at the rider, wheat-blond hair a dim, silvery tone in the darkness. "Goddamn," he spit out.

"Fargo," he heard her gasp in relief. "I was beginning to think I'd never find you."

"You'll wish you hadn't," he roared, putting the Colt down and rising to his feet. His hand shot out, yanked her to him. "I don't take to lies, especially ones all dressed up special," he said.

Her face grew stubborn. "I didn't lie to you," she said.

"And you didn't follow me. You're not here," he returned.

"I'm here, but I didn't lie to you," she said. "Somebody else did." His black brows stayed knitted together as he waited, his hand still holding her by the shirt. "The colonel has ordered the garrison to prepare to move out," she said.

Fargo slowly took his hand down, and the silence hung between them. "You sure of that?" he asked finally.

"I heard Lieutenant Smith ordering some of the men to get the supply wagon ready," she said.

"You could've heard wrong," Fargo ventured.

"No, I spoke to Lieutenant Smith. I insisted he tell me what was going on, and he did. I got the feeling he hasn't much confidence in the colonel and he's more than a little afraid," she said.

"He damn well ought to be," Fargo muttered. He turned from her, stared into the darkness. "That lying son of a bitch," he said. "That rotten, drunken bastard." He returned his eyes to Celia. She offered no disagreement.

"When I heard, I waited till almost dinnertime when I knew the colonel would be having his before-dinner drinks. I took the bay and raced from the fort. I'm sure he didn't see me," Celia said.

Fargo put his hand against her cheek. "I'm sorry I took off so at you," he said.

She rested her head against him. "I came as fast as I could," she said.

"How'd you find me?" he asked.

"A little memory, a lot of luck," she said. "I kept getting turned around, but I'd head north each time. I heard the waterfall and knew I was on the right track. Mostly I was lost and I just kept heading the right way by luck."

Fargo stepped back, and his mouth grew grim, his voice cold as a steel blade. "The bastard never intended to keep his word. That explains all his reasonableness, his change of heart," he bit out. He smashed his fist into the palm of his hand. "When is he pulling out, do you know?" he asked.

"Wednesday morning. Lieutenant Smith said they had to wait for the detachment to get back from Millerville to man the fort," she answered.

Fargo lowered himself onto the sleeping blanket. "Wednesday," he echoed, thinking aloud. "Then we don't have to start back till the morning. We can make it back by night." Celia came to kneel beside him. He saw the shiver go through her. "I'll build up the fire," he said.

"The sleeping blanket will be enough," she said. "With you in it." She undid buttons on the blouse, moved her hips in smooth quick half-circles, and in moments her round, lovely nakedness ducked under the blanket. He slid down beside her. "I don't like wasted nights," she said and caught the smile that touched his lips. She sat up on one elbow to peer at him. "I suppose you've heard that before," she said.

He nodded but didn't tell her how recently. He let his hands curl around her full breasts, and if she had further questions she forgot them at once. "Fargo . . . ah . . . ah . . . ah, yes," she murmured as he circled each tanned nipple with his thumb, traced the edges of each brown-pink little circle. He felt her move to lie on her back, her legs opening at once. "A quick learn, remember?" she breathed.

He answered with his pulsating organ, slowly sliding it along the little black triangle, and she shuddered in eagerness. She lifted her hips for him, the eternal invitation, and he felt her warm wetness close around him, flesh echoing words. The night would not be wasted.

6

They had ridden steadily through the day, stopping only for water and to let the horses rest. The night had come to close over the land when they neared the black outline of Fort Jasper. Celia had held up well, but now tiredness and tension turned her round-cheeked face into strained soberness. "How will you make him keep the bargain?" she asked as they rode toward the fort.

"Not by appealing to his sense of fair play," Fargo rasped.

"What then?" she pressed.

"By appealing to his sense of staying alive," Fargo said. "He'll stick to our agreement or I'll blow his damn drunken head off."

Celia frowned at him, her eyes staying on the hardness that had come into the intense, handsome face. "You mean that, don't you?" she murmured, a hushed shock in her voice.

"You're damn right I mean it," he said. He slowed the Ovaro as the two sentries at the gate stepped forward, rifles at the ready, their eyes scanning the two riders. They moved back and Fargo sent the horse forward. "I want to be alone with him," he said to Celia, and she nodded understanding. She turned the bay away from his side as they reached the long, low-roofed building of the officers' quarters and he watched her ride toward the stables. Dismounting, he took the single step to the colonel's quarters. A very young private standing guard moved to block his path to the door, the rifle held diagonally across his chest.

"Do you have an appointment with Colonel Kaster?" he asked in a voice that seemed to be still developing.

"Not exactly," Fargo said.

"Then you'll have to come back tomorrow. The colonel's not seeing anyone now," the trooper said.

Fargo's big Colt came to rest against his forehead, and the trooper's youthful face grew ashen. "I'll tell him you tried," Fargo said. "Now step aside." The trooper swallowed as he moved to one side, and Fargo pushed the door open to step into the colonel's quarters. Colonel Kaster paused with his glass in midair as he looked up at the big man with eyes that blazed blue fire, the Colt in one hand. Fargo saw Martha step in through the doorway of the next room, a dishtowel in one hand, her eyes wide with fear. He turned his eyes back to the colonel.

"You lying bastard," he growled. "You double-dealing son of a bitch."

The man put the glass down and let himself look aggrieved. "I changed my mind, that's all," he said. "I thought the matter over again and changed my mind."

"Like hell you did," Fargo said, stepping to the desk. "You planned to go ahead all along. You sold me a goddamn bill of goods."

"Don't you talk to me like that, mister," Colonel Kaster shouted, getting to his feet, his face darkening as he decided to use indignation as a weapon. Fargo's face remained as fixed as a stone carving.

"I'll talk to you any way I goddamn please, you lying

shithead," he said quietly. "You're going to call off your move or I'm going to blow your damn head off!"

"Fargo!" Martha's voice cut in, her cry full of fear.

"Shut up, Martha," the colonel snapped.

"Please, Fargo," she said.

"Shut up, Martha," Fargo echoed.

"You shoot me and you'll never reach the gate," the colonel said, and the arrogance in his voice couldn't cloak the uncertainty in the watery eyes.

"I'm not going to shoot you here," Fargo said almost mildly, raising the Colt in front of the man's face. "But you move this garrison out of here tomorrow morning and you can be sure that, somewhere along the way, you're going to be a dead man. You break our agreement and every bullet in this Colt will have your name on it."

Colonel Kaster's tongue flicked out over lips suddenly dry. "You can't threaten me, Fargo," he blustered, but the bold words wavered with weakness.

"That's no threat, colonel. That's just a statement of fact. You can count on it," Fargo said.

Colonel Kaster looked away from the blue-fire eyes that cut through him, lifted his glass of gin and lemon juice, and drained it in one long pull. His hand still trembled as he set it down. The room had grown silent except for the man's harsh breathing when the flurry of rifle shots broke the moment. Fargo turned to the door. Another volley of shots resounded from outside, and then running feet, shouts of alarm. The colonel swerved around the desk and ran outside into the dark of the compound, Fargo following, dropping the Colt back in its holster. A dozen troopers were atop the wooden platform behind the fort fence, three letting go with another round of fire.

"What's going on here?" the colonel shouted, and Fargo saw the men halt, others emerge from the barracks to look on. One young trooper climbed down from the platform. "Indians, sir, five of them," he said. "Three of them sneaked close in on foot and started firing arrows. Then another two ran in low from the other side."

"Did you get any of them?" the colonel asked.

"Don't think so, sir. They just ran in and ran out," the trooper said. Fargo saw Lieutenant Smith hurrying toward him, an arrow and a piece of parchment in one hand.

"They left this, sir," the lieutenant called to the colonel. "Shot it into the gate with this arrow."

Colonel Kaster took the sheet of parchment, frowned down at it, and Fargo suddenly noticed Celia almost at his elbow, the door to her quarters open behind her. Her eyes met his in a brief, wordless exchange.

"Look at this, now," the Colonel said. "One of them learned to write some English." He held the parchment out to Fargo, and the Trailsman scanned the big, child-like scrawl on the parchment.

" 'Try take women by Red Mountain River,' " he read aloud.

He frowned down at the parchment until the colonel drew it back. Fargo saw a half-sneer of triumph on the man's face. "There's your answer, Fargo. He's using the women as bait. He's defying me to rescue them," the colonel said.

"That much seems plain enough," Fargo said.

"That's what it is, a challenge," the Colonel said.

"There's more to it," Fargo said.

"Wait in my quarters. We'll finish discussing this there," the colonel ordered. Fargo shot a quick glance at Celia and walked back to the Colonel's quarters, ignoring Martha's eyes as he brushed past her. The Colonel was talking to Lieutenant Smith, he noted as he went inside. Martha followed him in, seemed to grope for the right words. Fargo's silence was stony, and a few moments later the Colonel strode in, the parchment in his hand.

"This changes everything," he said.

"It changes nothing," Fargo shot back. "He's tossed out the bait and he's waiting for you to take it. There's something more behind it."

"You insist on giving him more credit than he deserves," the Colonel said.

"You insist on giving him less."

"It's a challenge, nothing more. The fool has grown overconfident," the Colonel said. "He'll learn his lesson the hard way."

Fargo's frown was made of incredulity. "Overconfident my ass," he roared. "He tossed out the bait because he knew you'd have to take it. He knew word of it would get to the settlers damn quick and they'd insist you try to save their women."

"And I will save them. He'll learn something about proper military tactics," the Colonel said with infuriating pomposity.

"Dammit, it's not that simple. There's more behind it. It's not his way to toss out a head-to-head challenge," Fargo said. "I still need the time to find out what he's planning. Even more lives depend on it now. Our agreement still holds." He fastened the Colonel with eyes cold as blue ice. "And if I don't get it, the rest still stands, too. Six bullets still have your name on them," he growled. He turned and strode to the door, glanced back. The Colonel seemed improperly calm, but then the man had practiced wearing many kinds of masks for too many years. Fargo pulled the door open and strode outside. He saw Lieutenant Smith with six troopers standing almost at attention and started past them.

"You're under arrest, sir," he heard the lieutenant say. He spun, his hand moving toward the Colt. He pulled it back as he saw the six army carbines leveled at him. The lieutenant's young face looked apologetic. "Colonel's orders, sir," he said as he reached past the big man and took the Colt from the holster. Fargo heard the door open behind him and saw Colonel Kaster emerge, his mouth twisted in a smile of sneering triumph.

"Lock him up. I'll file formal charges later," the colonel said. Fargo felt the prod of a rifle barrel and the six troopers boxed him. He was moved along as he held all his curses seething inside himself.

The jailhouse occupied the far end of the long barracks building, and he saw he was the only occupant as he was locked into one of two cells. He watched the lieutenant lock his revolver into the top drawer of a wooden cabinet in the outer area of the jail. The cell held a hard cot against one wall, and a small, barred window let him look out on the darkened compound. The trooper on guard duty sat on a long chair in the small outer area. He wore a standard army sidearm at his waist and regarded Fargo with mild curiosity. "Don't get many civilians in here," he remarked.

"Let me out and we'll have a party," Fargo said as his stomach churned. He lay down on the hard cot after examining every inch of the tiny cell. It was sturdy, all too sturdy. He found a tin cup under the cot. "How about some water?" he called and saw the trooper pick up a white ceramic pitcher from the top of the cabinet. The man approached the cell.

"Hold the cup out through the bars," he ordered, and waited till Fargo had almost his entire arm stretched out before pouring the water into the cup. He had been well trained, Fargo swore silently as he drew the cup back into the cell and drank from it. He lay down on the cot again, felt the helpless fury surging inside himself. He hadn't underestimated the self-serving desperation of the man, only his duplicity, and he swore at himself for that. Helplessness was not a condition he'd much experience with, and he railed at the totality of it, wanted to rise up and smash his fists against the cell walls. But he fought down the impulse. Wasting strength and energy was perhaps satisfying but self-defeating. He forced himself to stop the churning fury inside him and closed his eyes, finally slept some in fitful spurts.

He snapped awake as he heard the guard's voice, saw the dawn pushing itself through the window. He sat up, peered outside at the entrance area. Another trooper was taking over, he saw. The changing of the guard, he noted bitterly. He went to the window and peered out. The garrison was turning out, horses being readied, the supply wagon already drawn up. They'd be ready to pull out soon. He was taking damn near the full garrison, Fargo saw, leaving only a skeleton force at the fort. He turned away as he heard other voices at the doorway to the jail and saw the colonel enter. His eyes sought out the man, peering at the arrogantly weak face. The colonel had already had a drink, he smelled, as the man approached his cell. The colonel's courage, like everything else about him, came out of a bottle.

"I'll tend to you when I get back," the colonel said. "You should have cooperated with me, Fargo."

"Go to hell," Fargo growled.

"You're the kind that can't admit being wrong," the man sneered. "This will be no contest. You'll see."

Fargo met the man's superior gaze. "You're right on that," he said and saw the colonel's eyebrows lift. "A Crow warrior chief who's planned every move perfectly, who leads a force of superb fighting men, who's holding some kind of trump card against a garrison of inexperienced boys led by a drunken asshole. It's no contest, as you said."

116

He saw the colonel's mouth quiver. "When I get back I'll find a way to put you before a firing squad," the man hissed.

"If you've enough men left for a firing squad," Fargo said.

Colonel Kaster whirled and strode from the jail. Fargo waited a moment, returned to the window, and saw the full garrison mounted and ready to move. The colonel took his place at the head of one column, sitting a dark-brown gelding, and Fargo saw Lieutenant Smith at the head of the other column. He let his eyes move across the troopers, most so very young, their faces set with what seemed a combination of determination and apprehension. The Colonel raised his hand. "Move out," Lieutenant Smith called, and Fargo watched as the two columns left, winding their way out of the fort, the supply wagon at the rear.

He turned from the barred window and again knew the fury of helplessness. Colonel Henry Kaster could commit suicide for all he cared, but he was taking a garrison of young, inexperienced troopers with him. And those poor women who had endured in hope of deliverance. Somewhere, somehow, the Crow had a final welcome prepared and waiting. Fargo smashed his fist into his hand and cursed aloud. He'd just turned to the barred door when he saw the figure enter the jailhouse, wheat-blond hair enclosed in a blue kerchief. She wore a dark-blue shirt and a matching skirt, and she carried a small tray of dishes covered by a cloth. The trooper stood up at once.

"I've brought breakfast for the prisoner," she said. "May I go into the cell and talk?"

"No, ma'am," the trooper said politely but firmly. "You'll have to talk to him from outside the bars. But we can slip the tray in." He came to the cell and opened a small slot cut out of the bars at one side that proved just

117

large enough for Celia to slide the tray through. Fargo took the tray, and the trooper returned to his chair. Celia positioned herself against the bars so as to block the trooper's direct gaze. Her eyes were signaling something that told him to be prepared.

"Did you sleep any?" she asked.

"Not much," he answered.

"I made the coffee just the way you like it, with chicory in it," she said.

"Thanks," he answered, lifting the towel and picking up the coffee mug. His eyes stayed on her as he sipped the hot brew.

"I'm sorry about all this," she said, keeping up the bland conversation. "I'm sure it'll all work out."

"I hope so," he said, his eyes staying on hers.

"I'll be leaving soon," she went on, and he saw her hand slowly move to the dark-blue shirt, her fingers unbutton the two middle buttons. The smooth curve of her breasts pushed forward at once as the blouse came open. But her fingers drew out something else, a small pistol. "I'll be going back to Kansas," she went on as she pushed it through the bars at him, keeping her back blocking the trooper's vision. Fargo took the little revolver and pushed it into his pocket. "You have any messages for anyone back in Kansas?" Celia asked.

"Not now," he answered. "And I'm not very hungry, either." He kept one hand in his pocket, fingered the little revolver, the kind often called a lady's gun. He felt the inlaid stock, the twin barrels, drew his thumb over the hammer and pulled it back. Larger than a derringer, it was no doubt European-made, with a center-fire rimmed cartridge. He smiled to himself. A highly limited little item but effective at the right time and in the right place. This would be a new place for its use, he noted wryly.

Celia stepped back from the bars and called the

trooper. "Would you please take the tray?" she asked, and the soldier came at once. As he bent over to open the little slot, Fargo drew the little pistol from his pocket, pushed it between the bars into the trooper's face. He saw the man's eyes widen in surprise.

"Don't move, soldier," Fargo said softly. "This is a little gun, but it's big enough to put two holes in the middle of your forehead." The soldier's young face grew pale, and he stayed bent over, his eyes almost crossed as he stared into the tiny twin barrels of the pistol. "Take the keys from his back pocket, Celia," Fargo said, keeping the little gun in the man's face. Celia extracted the cell keys deftly from the soldier's pocket, opened the cell door without trouble, and Fargo straightened, kept the little pistol trained on the man as he stepped from the cell. "Straighten up, soldier," he said. "Into the cell." The trooper obeyed, and Fargo took the towel from the tray and fashioned a makeshift gag for the man. He found a short piece of rope and tied the soldier's hands behind his back. "Somebody will find you soon enough," he said as he closed the cell door on the man.

He pulled the top drawer open, breaking the weak lock on the cabinet, and retrieved his Colt. "I've the Ovaro and my bay just outside the compound," Celia said. "We just walk across the compound together. Hold my arm. I don't think hardly any of these men left even know you were in there."

Fargo took Celia's arm and stepped outside with her, casually began to cross the compound. They drew only a few stray glances and turned as they went through the gate, the two horses tethered just outside the wall. "I owe you again," Fargo said as he swung onto the Ovaro.

"Where do we go now?" she asked, and he smiled at the question.

"Still trying?" he asked. "I told you, you can't do it."

"One last time," she said.

"It could be that," he warned.

She nodded. "But I can't sit around waiting. It's too much with me, now."

"Let's ride," he said and wheeled the Ovaro in a tight circle.

"North?" she asked, catching up to him.

"North," he repeated. "I still think there's another camp with the answers."

"Where's Red Mountain River?" Celia asked.

"West of the waterfall. It'll take the garrison another full day longer to reach it. It gives us that much time, and we'll sure as hell need it," Fargo said. He broke off further talk by increasing the pace, riding hard until he halted in the afternoon to let the horses rest and drink at a stream. "We've made good time. We'll be past the waterfall before dark," he said as Celia sat beside him on the grass.

"What if you can't find that other camp? Or what if there isn't one?" Celia asked.

"We still ride like hell to intercept the garrison before they reach Red Mountain River. Camp or no camp, they're riding into something. Hawkwing's not overconfident. He's too smart for that," Fargo said.

"Uncle Henry didn't listen to you before. What makes you think he'll listen now?" she questioned.

"He'll listen," Fargo said grimly. "Let's ride." He continued to set the driving pace, slowing only when night came. When he finally halted they were but a few hours from Hawkwing's camp. Celia slept at once in his arms, and he had to wake her when morning came. He found a large cluster of pink roses and gathered enough of the haws or rose hips to provide a wild breakfast. "We eat while we ride," he said, determined to make every second

120

count. The land began to turn into the now-familiar long slopes with good wooded cover, and he halted when they reached the last of the slopes before the Crow camp. Leaving the horses where they'd tethered them last time, they proceeded on foot again and then on their bellies up to the last ridge that overlooked the camp.

Fargo heard Celia's gasp of surprise as she lay beside him, peering down at the camp below. The two tipis remained, but the camp was deserted. "They've gone," she breathed.

"On their way to Red Mountain River," Fargo said.

"Did you expect this?" Celia frowned.

"I figured it might be," he told her. "But then they could still have been here."

"Does this mean we can't find the other camp?" she asked.

"It could help us," he said, and she frowned back. "I'll get the horses and we'll go down and look around," he said, not answering her frown. Retrieving the two mounts, he rode slowly down the slope into the still camp and dismounted. He squatted down and studied the marks on the ground as Celia wandered through the camp. He rose, followed a set of tracks, reading the soil as other men read a book. "They haven't been gone more than a day," he said.

"This is Judy's," he heard Celia call and saw her holding up a length of pink hair ribbon. She stood in front of one of the tipis. He saw her pull the flap of the tipi open and start inside, and he had just returned his attention to the ground when her scream exploded the silence of the abandoned camp. He whirled, Colt in hand instantly, saw Celia falling backward out of the tipi, and then he saw the thin, emaciated, wrinkled old form half-atop her. The old squaw, one thin but sinewy arm upraised, clasped strong fingers around a bone knife. Celia fell to the ground screaming, tried to twist away, trying to defend herself more than fight back, but the old crone clung to her as a spider clings to a leaf, gray-white hair in disarray, her deerskin garment flapping loosely, as though there were no body inside it.

Fargo saw the old crone start to plunge the bone knife downward, and his finger tightened on the trigger. The big Colt barked, the shot slamming directly into the old squaw's chest. She flew backward as though a giant wind had suddenly picked her up and tossed her away. She struck the ground face down, and Fargo reached Celia in two long strides, pulled her to her feet. He stared with her at the object on the ground, something that seemed nothing more than an old deerskin crumpled together with a stringy, gray rag.

"She was inside," Celia breathed. "I didn't even see her until she flew at me." She leaned against Fargo, shuddered. He pushed her to stand alone.

"Stay here," he said and poked his head inside the tipi, emerged, and did the same with the other one. "Nobody else," he said, returning to Celia.

"What was she doing in there?" Celia asked.

"Waiting to die," he said and saw the shock in Celia's eyes. "She was obviously unable to make the trip with the others. In many Indian cultures, the old are left to die alone, to wait the coming of the Great Spirit surrounded by nature."

"She certainly seemed strong enough to me," Celia commented.

"A last effort, a last surge of strength," Fargo said and suddenly saw the small red stain at the side of the dark-blue shirt. "Sit down," he said as he began to unbutton the shirt, and Celia looked down at herself.

"My God," she gasped as he pulled the shirt back and

her breasts pushed forward. The side of her left breast was trickling blood.

"It's only a scrape," he said, examining the soft, lovely mound. "You were lucky. Those bone knives can make a nasty wound." He rose, went to his saddlebag, and took some St. Johnswort oil from a little vial. He applied it gently to the scrape. "Great for bruises and scrapes," he murmured. "Sit for a few moments until it soaks in and dries." He rose, looked down at her as she sat back on her elbows, the shirt pulled to the sides and the beautifully formed, tanned breasts curving upward invitingly. He turned away from the hint of a smile on her lips and cursed the time they didn't have, forced his concentration to return to studying the ground. He walked to the edge of the camp, grunted at what he read. "Button up and bring the horses," he called as he knelt on the ground. Celia was at his side in a few moments, and he pointed to the marks that led from the edge of the camp into the woodland.

"They headed west, for Red Mountain river," he said. "They kept the captives tied together, walked them in single file. The old squaws followed up behind."

"All but one," Celia murmured.

"Mount up. We've a trail to follow," Fargo said.

"But they're heading toward the Red Mountain meeting place. What about the other camp?" she questioned.

"We might just find it yet," he said as he led the way into the woods. The trail was fresh and large enough to make it easy to follow, and he increased his usual tracking pace. The day had slipped into late afternoon when he reined to a halt, swung from the pinto to kneel on the ground, his hands pressing lightly on the earth, his fingers tracing along the marks in the soil. He rose, walked from the trail, a sharp right turn, then came back to Celia. "The old squaws left the others here. One brave on horseback went with them," he said. "I expected this might happen. They'd be no use at Red Mountain River."

He climbed onto the pinto and began to follow the trail of the old squaws that had turned sharply, led north again. They had kept an almost straight line, he saw, their tiredness seen in the way their moccasined prints began to scuff along the ground. Night fell, the dense forest making the trail impossible to see in the dim, filtered moonlight. "They've held it straight all along. A straight line saves tired legs and feet. I'm going to bet they won't change," he said, moved the pinto forward. He picked his way through the blackness of the woods, staying in a straight line. They rode through another hour, and partway into the next. Then he halted the pinto, put his hand onto Celia's bridle. The sound drifted toward him, very faint, but the unmistakable sound of drums. He leaned forward in the saddle, his ears straining.

"Drums," Celia offered.

"Not just drums. War drums," he grunted. He moved forward, letting the sound of the drums guide him. They grew louder quickly, but he stayed in the saddle until the glow of large campfires reached into the forest, the sounds of the drums and the chanting voices filling the dark. He halted, dismounted, and waited for Celia to come beside him before moving forward in a crouch to finally halt behind a screen of coarse boxelder leaves.

The camp stretched out before him, twenty tipis, he estimated, a longhouse in the distance. Squaws, young and old, naked children, drying racks, everything that stamped it as the main camp. Celia's fingers dug into his arm as she followed his eyes to the foreground of the fires where the almost naked bucks danced to the rhythm of the large two-headed drums. "There are hundreds of them," Celia breathed in shock and awe.

The guess was too accurate, Fargo grimaced. "And all

in war paint, which means they'll set out come morning," he muttered.

"Set out for Red Mountain River?" Celia said.

He didn't answer at once, his mind racing, putting pieces together, becoming a Crow warrior again. Hawkwing, the captive women, and a smaller force of braves would reach Red Mountain River within another day. They'd set up their positions, the bait prominently displayed. The garrison would take another day to reach them. Fargo's eyes narrowed as he watched the powerful force of Crow bucks, their painted faces and bodies glowing in the light of the fire.

"Timing," he said to Celia, his voice filled with bitter admiration. "They'll reach the Red Mountain River right after the garrison. The colonel will commit his entire force attacking the Crow holding the captives. It'll seem like a sizable number to him, but they'll show just enough to draw him in."

"And this main force will sweep up from behind," Celia said.

"Bull's-eye," Fargo bit out. "They'll have surprise and numbers and experience. Those green troopers won't know which way to turn. It'll be a slaughter." He half rose, started to back away from the edge of the camp, pulling Celia with him. He stayed silent till he reached the horses, pulled himself into the saddle. "There's one chance," he said. "We have to intercept the garrison. We'll camp tonight, give the horses a solid night's rest, and ride like hell tomorrow. I'm pretty sure which way the garrison will take to reach Red Mountain River. They'll halt come sundown tomorrow night and reach the river the next morning ready to fight."

"And if we intercept them?"

"We'll have four or five hours to figure a way to avoid

a slaughter," Fargo said. "Let's find a place to bed down."

He turned the pinto and rode back through the deep dark of the woods, and finally the sound of the war drums faded away. He found a spot against a flat outcrop of malachite with enough good grazing grass for the horses. He slipped into his bedroll, and Celia was beside him at once. He felt her lips on his chest, tiny nibbling sensations. Her round little belly came over to rest across him. "I'm too on edge to sleep," she murmured.

"We'll have to do something about that," he said as he felt himself stiffening against the soft mound of belly.

"Aaaah," she breathed at once, began to rub up and down over him, and then, with almost desperate abruptness, she slipped downward, then up, pushing herself onto the waiting, rigid magnet, and he felt the urgent desperation in her. He took her harshly, almost roughly, but her cries were of pleasure, not protest. Her rounded body clung to him, pressing, rubbing, caressing, and the urgency in her persisted, became a thing of surprising frenzy. "Yes, more, oh, yes, more, Fargo, more, more . . . aaaiiiii . . . oh, God," she breathed, and only when he brought her to that moment of exploding surcease did her cries end.

She lay beside him asleep almost at once, and he wondered if she really understood that it could have been her last orgasm.

7

In the morning he set a hard-riding pace and held it through the day, cutting across country, turning to take advantage of every path and passage that offered even the smallest shortcut, his goal a narrow stretch of flatland that ran alongside the hills. It was the only good route to Red Mountain River for a full garrison with a supply wagon. He halted four times to let the horses drink and catch their breath, and as dusk began to slide its violet shawl over the land he saw the strain showing on Celia's face. He halted as they started to go through a stand of timber.

"The garrison ought to be camping somewhere just the other side of this line of trees," he told her. "You can wait here and I'll send back for you if you don't want to come with me."

"Why wouldn't I want to come with you?" She frowned.

His eyes grew hard as blue quartz. "Because I might just blow your Uncle Henry's head off," Fargo growled. "I've had it with him, and there's no more time, not for the captives, not for that garrison of green troopers, and not for him. Especially not for him."

He saw her search his eyes and realize he meant every word of what he'd said. She swallowed, and her voice was small. "I'll go with you," she said. "Maybe I can make him listen."

Fargo shrugged. It was just possible. The man was weak, his bravado only a hollow mask. He was driven by forces within himself he could no longer control or understand. A bottle, not a carbine, was his real weapon, his courage and his shield. Perhaps Celia's presence would have its effect. He was willing to take any outside chance. He moved forward through the line of trees, reached the other side quickly, enough daylight still on the land to see the garrison camped a few dozen yards ahead along the side of the flat passage. He turned the pinto to move through the trees till he was abreast of the camp, let his eyes scan the scene.

The troopers showed their tiredness, most stretched out on the ground. He found Colonel Kaster, half lying on a blanket near the trees where he waited. The man took a deep draft out of a canteen. The way he swallowed, exhaled afterward, the satisfaction in his face, all revealed that the canteen held something other than water. Fargo slid from the pinto, moved silently along the treeline toward the man. He flicked a quick glance at those nearest, saw Lieutenant Smith sitting cross-legged, finishing his rations. Two line sergeants sat with him. Another lieutenant lay half asleep against his saddle a few yards away.

Fargo cast a glance at Celia. She watched him with her eyes wide, dismay and anxiety in the light-brown pupils. He bent low as he came directly opposite the figure of Colonel Kaster and suddenly, moving with the silent spring of a cougar, he pushed from the trees, reached the colonel before the man had chance to focus his eyes on him. The big Colt pressed into the colonel's temple, and Fargo saw the man's watery eyes grow even paler.

"Get up," Fargo growled. "I don't like to kill a man sitting down."

"Now, hold, Fargo," Colonel Kaster muttered as he pushed himself to his feet. "I'm sure we can work out something."

"You rotten, weak-kneed bastard," Fargo said, letting his voice grow louder. He saw Lieutenant Smith get to his feet, the two sergeants with him. The other officer started to come nearer, and Fargo watched a dozen troopers become aware of his presence.

"Nobody do anything. This man is insane," the colonel said, and the fear was hard in his voice.

Fargo kept the Colt pressed against the man's temple. For emphasis, he pulled the hammer back as he let his eyes sweep those who were quickly gathering around. "This drunken incompetent is leading you into a wholesale slaughter, every last one of you," Fargo said. "You've been set up. The women are only bait. There's a war party of maybe two hundred Crows riding this way. While this alcoholic has you attacking the force with the captives, they're going to hit you from behind and kill every last one of you."

"Ask him how he knows all this," the colonel called to the young officer, the sneer heavy in his voice, and Fargo saw the question reflect in Smith's eyes.

"Because I saw them. I found the other camp. I've been telling this damn fool all along to hold off. I knew Hawkwing was planning something more than grabbing off some women captives," Fargo said.

"He's lying. He'll say anything to keep me from taking Hawkwing. He wants that for himself," the colonel shouted.

"He's not lying," a voice cut in, and Fargo saw Celia move out from the trees astride the bay.

"*Celia!*" the colonel gasped.

"I was with him. I saw them," Celia said.

"Don't listen to her. She'll say anything he wants her to say," the colonel cut in. "She's in with him."

"Please, Uncle Henry, don't keep on with this terrible thing," Celia said. "Fargo's been right all along, and now he's just trying to stop you from leading all these men into a massacre."

"You stay out of things that don't concern you," the man shouted at her.

Fargo pushed the barrel of the Colt harder into the colonel's temple as he half turned to face Smith. "Lieutenant, you've been serving under this man and looking the other way, but you know what he is. You take command of this troop and I'll try to help you save your necks."

He watched the young officer hesitate, his eyes moving to the others. They gave back concern, indecision, confusion, all understandable enough, Fargo realized. The colonel seized the moment at once. "I'll have any man who takes part in this court-martialed for mutiny," he shouted.

Fargo slowly scanned the others, his eyes pausing meaningfully at each man, rested his gaze on Lieutenant Smith. "Maybe he'll court-martial all of you. The Crow are sure as hell going to kill you if you go along with him. Your choice, soldier," he said grimly. The long moment seemed endless, and he watched as the young officer let his breath out in a long sigh, turned his gaze on the colonel.

"I can't see Mr. Fargo, and your own niece, coming all this way just to make up stories," the lieutenant said. "And, meaning no disrespect, sir, but I always felt you weren't much fit to command. I'm going to go along with Mr. Fargo."

"I'll have you before a firing squad for this," Colonel Kaster roared.

"I'm taking command of this garrison by reason of your unfitness, sir," Smith said very firmly. He glanced at the other troopers. "Anyone object?" Their silence was his answer.

Fargo lifted the sidearm from the colonel's holster belt, tossed it to one of the sergeants. Colonel Kaster sank down to the ground, reached for his canteen, and drank quickly, inhaled a deep breath when he finished and drew a cloak of bluster around himself. "You'll pay for this, all of you," he flung out.

Fargo's face was grave. "I expect we will, one way or the other," he said and moved to where Celia had dismounted. He saw the lieutenant detail two troopers to guard the colonel and waited as the young officer brought two of his sergeants over to him.

"You said you'd try to help us," Smith reminded him.

Fargo nodded, dropped down to one knee on the ground. Using the end of a stick, he drew a diagram in the soil as the lieutenant and a dozen of the other troopers watched. "There are two parts to this operation, now. They've got to work together. One is to save the women. The other is to avoid being massacred. We've one advantage. The main force of the Crow will come riding full out, figuring they'll come up behind you as you're attacking to save the women. That's what we've got to use against them."

"How?" one of the sergeants asked as Fargo finished drawing his diagram.

"Right here, about a half-mile from the river, the road cuts through a section of rocks on both sides, not huge rocks but just right for an ambush," Fargo said.

"We'll be waiting as they come roaring through and hit them from both sides," Smith said.

"Right. It'll be your one chance. You'll do the surpris-

ing. Hit them hard. Pour it into them and you'll even the
odds before they get a chance to take cover," Fargo said.

"What about the women at the river?" Smith asked.

"I'll need thirty of your men, the wagon, and a trooper
to drive it. I'll have to carry out that attack. First, to try
to save the captives, and second, if the main Crow force
doesn't hear the attack they'll smell something wrong right
away. I want enough men to keep up a steady barrage
they'll be sure to hear and come on thinking their plan is
working."

"Understood," the lieutenant said crisply.

"Soon as we hear your fire and finish the attack, your
troopers can hightail it back to you," Fargo said.

"I hope so. I know I'll be needing them. But Hawkwing is waiting at the river. What if his force pins you
down?" Smith asked.

Fargo stared into the night for a long moment, his eyes
narrowed in thought. "No, that's not in the cards," he
said finally. Smith waited but Fargo added no more and
turned to Celia. "You'll be coming with me. I'll want you
to see to the women, as many as we can save," he said.

"Thirty men. I'll have Sergeant O'Neill pick the squad
for you by morning," Smith said.

"Now," Fargo replied. "I'm moving out now."

He saw the lieutenant's brows lift, but the man had already learned the big, black-haired man said only as
much as he wanted to say. "You heard Mr. Fargo," Smith
said to a broad-faced trooper. "Get thirty men, the
wagon, and a driver ready to move out."

"Yes, sir," the sergeant said and hurried away.

Fargo saw the colonel lower the canteen from his lips,
a sneer staining his face as he looked up at the lieutenant
and the others. "You're letting this man use you," he said.

"I'm expecting to use you come morning, sir," Smith
said. "We'll need every gun we can get."

"What damned nerve," the colonel roared. "I'm not serving under any mutineering junior officer."

Fargo smiled inwardly. Smith was a good man. He stayed firm and unflustered. "Your choice, sir," the lieutenant said. "I don't think the Crow will care." He turned away and strode to the other officers and sergeants to confer on tactics. Celia moved to Fargo with the Ovaro, and the Trailsman's face was grim as he took the reins of the horse. He looked past her and saw Sergeant O'Neill leading the thirty men toward him.

Fargo swung onto the Ovaro as he scanned the sergeant and the squad of troopers. "We'll ride slow and easy, mostly at a walk," he told Sergeant O'Neill. "I'll fill you in on the rest when it's time."

The sergeant nodded, and Fargo led the squad forward, the troopers riding in a column of twos. Celia stayed alongside the Trailsman and watched his eyes sweep the land that was barely lighted by a new moon, his glances taking in passage and roadside, brush and timber, and she rode in silence beside him, very aware of the grimness that cloaked his tall, straight figure. Not till she caught his gesture when they reached the place where rocks lined the road did she speak.

"We're getting near the river, then," she said, and he nodded. "The lieutenant asked what if Hawkwing pinned you down at the river and you said it wasn't in the cards. What is in the cards, Fargo?" she asked.

He shot her a hard glance. "Contempt. A last gesture, a final twist," he said.

"Meaning what exactly?" she prodded.

Fargo's jaws stayed tight. "He's planned his every move. He's pulled the strings all along. So far as he knows, it's going just as he expects. The colonel's going to charge in to the attack to save the captives. But Hawkwing will leave no one to save." Fargo saw Celia's eyes stare at him, her smooth brow furrowed. "By now he's given orders to kill every one of the women the minute the attack begins," Fargo said and heard Celia's sharp gasp. "The saviors will have a victory that will be no victory at all. He'll have tricked them and cheated them and he'll be laughing as he slips away, circles, and goes back to join the main force attacking from behind."

Celia rode in a kind of stunned silence until he reined to a halt. "Can you do anything?" she asked, despair in the question.

"Maybe. I'm sure as hell going to try," he told her and swung from the saddle. "On foot now," he said to Sergeant O'Neill. "They'll be there, waiting. I don't want to wake them up." The sergeant nodded, gave the troop hand signals to dismount. Fargo cast a glance upward at the new moon, saw it was far down its trackless path in the sky. Another hour till dawn. Enough time, he grunted as he moved forward. The road became less of a road, and soon he pushed his way through very heavy growths of spicebush with some taller shadbush interspersed. The brush would afford good cover, he grunted in satisfaction. But for Hawkwing as well.

He paused, sniffed the air, his nostrils flaring to catch the scent of the river, a scent made of wet riverbank, damp grass, and shore reeds. He halted, turned to the sergeant almost at his elbow. "You and five men," he said. "The rest wait here." The sergeant beckoned to five of the troopers, and Fargo moved forward, Celia at his side, as he left the pinto with the other horses. He pushed his way through the spicebush until he saw the river, the towering bulk of Red Mountain rising up behind it, and he sank to one knee as the sergeant and Celia came up beside him. On the other side of the river, not far in from the bank, he saw the women, lined up in a row, each tied to a stake driven in the ground. The Crow chieftain had put them in plain view, a mocking invitation. It also made it easier to put an arrow through each one, he cursed silently.

He turned to the five troopers, let his glance go from man to man. "Here's the plan," he began. "First we go downriver and cross over, then make our way back up the other side. I'm going to try to cut the women free so they won't be held in place against those stakes when the fighting starts. That means the bucks assigned to kill them won't be able to stay behind cover and just put an arrow into each. They'll have to get in close with a knife or tomahawk to do the job." He paused and saw the men nod in understanding. "You five are going to put a bullet into every buck that tries to reach them. That's all you're going to do. Forget the rest of the battle, forget the other bucks no matter how clear a shot you might have at one. You concentrate on those women and any Crow that tries to reach them. Got it?"

"Yes, sir," one of the troopers said. "But they'll know something is wrong right away. Maybe they won't try."

"They'll try. They have to," Fargo said. "They've been given an important thing to do. Honor, obedience, their place as braves, all depend on it. They'll try." He turned to Sergeant O'Neill. "You'll lead the attack come morning," he said. "When you hear me fire one shot, you lay down a barrage at anything with red skin. Pour in the fire. We want the main Crow force coming up to hear it and think everything's going according to plan. I don't know how much return fire you'll get here."

He saw the sergeant's eyebrows lift. "You don't know?"

"That's right. Hawkwing will see something's gone wrong. I expect he'll slip away and ride to join up with his main force," Fargo said. He turned back to the five troopers. "Clean out your pockets," he said. "Keys, watches, loose change, anything that can rattle. Give it to the sergeant."

As the men obeyed he turned to Celia and met her wide, grave eyes. "You stay with the wagon. If it goes well, I'll have the women put into the wagon," he said.

"And if it doesn't go well?" she murmured.

His smile was wry. "It'll be a long time between drinks," he said, kissed her lightly. "Or between anything else."

He turned, nodded to the five troopers, and they fell in line behind him as he set off in a loping crouch. He led the way downriver perhaps half a mile before halting and lowering himself into the water. The troopers followed, in single file, holding their rifles out of the water. He led the way slowly, his feet edging through the soft bottom until he couldn't touch any longer, and then he let himself float. He reached the other side of the river a dozen yards down from where he'd entered and crawled onto the bank and rested as he waited for the five troopers to pull themselves from the water. He gave them five minutes to rest, then began to move back along the riverbank, staying in the spicebush, inching forward, moving more slowly than he might have alone, aware that those following hadn't his skills in moving silently through the brush. Minutes seemed to drag heavily, but he resisted the amateur's temptation to hurry. Suddenly he dropped to one knee as he spied the woman and the stake directly ahead, motioned for the others to do the same.

His eyes peered at the woman tied to the stake, followed the line of the other captives beyond her. His glance went skyward where he saw the moon was no longer visible. Dawn was close, he realized unhappily. Time was growing short. He inched forward a little farther, and now he could hear the sounds of sleep from the brush farther in from the shoreline, heavy, rhythmic breathing and guttural snores. He looked back at the five troopers and motioned for them to lower themselves to the ground. They did so and brought their rifles up into firing position. He glanced down the line of stakes and the bound captives, motioned again to the troopers, and they shifted on their stomachs to give each man his own line of vision covering the stakes.

Fargo turned, drew the double-edged throwing knife from its sheath around his calf. His hand firmly on the hilt, he started forward, alone now, dropped to his stomach, and began to crawl snakelike across the grass. The bulk of the sleeping Crow were to his right in the brush, and he edged closer to the first woman, pausing every few feet to look and listen. He could see the woman clearly now, middle-aged, now looking old, her body sagging against the stake. Fargo started forward again when he froze as the bush in front of him moved and he saw the Indian rise from it, peer into the darkness. He was posted as sentry, plainly, and he slowly began to turn in a half-circle, a frown on his face as he peered into the dark. He hadn't been heard, he was certain, Fargo pondered. The Indian was up and suddenly suspicious out of a sixth sense, a feeling of danger, the acuteness of the wild.

Fargo's arm rose and he drew powerful leg muscles together. There was no time to think about savagery turned around. There was time only to strike. Only the faintest movement of brush sounded as he catapulted forward, his arm coming down with the speed of a rattler's strike. The Crow spun around but only in time to meet the blade that sank to its hilt in his thorax. His mouth opened soundlessly, gulped in air as he clutched at the object imbedded into his flesh. Fargo caught him as he started to fall, lowered him silently to the ground. He yanked the pencil-thin throwing knife free, remained on one knee, his eyes sweeping the area, his ears straining. But no other form moved, and Fargo rose to a half-crouch, reached the woman at the nearest stake in one stride, and clapped a hand over her mouth. He felt her body stiffen as he held his hand tight to her face. "Don't talk. Just listen," he breathed into her ear. "Do you hear me?"

The woman nodded, and he removed his hand and began to cut the ropes binding her arms to the stake. "Don't move," he whispered. "Keep your arms just where they are, as if you were still tied." The woman nodded again. "When the shooting starts, you drop to the ground. Don't try to run. Just drop in place and stay there. Understand?" he breathed. "You want to stay alive, you do exactly what I say." Once more the woman nodded, and he was at the next stake in one long stride, found a young girl whose head had turned to see him with wide eyes. He repeated the same terse message as he severed her bonds and received a nod of understanding. He moved on, from stake to stake, pausing between each to scan the brush where the Indians still slept. He gave the same message to each woman, and when he reached the last of them the sky was lightening. It had taken him longer than he'd hoped, but Hawkwing had posted only one sentry. It was the Indian's only excursion into overconfidence, and he'd pay for it, Fargo murmured in grim silence. He moved back, sank into the spicebush, and sheathed the knife. The new day came on quickly now, as if hurrying to announce itself. He lay waiting, his eyes traveling along the line of stakes. None of the women had moved, he saw with satisfaction, and a wave of bitterness swept over him as he wondered how many would finally make it through alive. All, he hoped, even as he knew that was little more than wishful thinking.

The day grew lighter when he saw the brush move behind the line of stakes. A Crow appeared, then another and then more. They moved around the ends of the line of stakes, bows in hand, eyes fastened on the shoreline directly across the river. Fargo stayed a silent, unseen presence and watched as more near-naked figures emerged from the brush to move closer to the riverbank. He glimpsed still others appear but stay back in the heavy brush. He guessed there were twenty or so and was wondering about Hawkwing when he saw the Indian pony move slowly through the brush and halt, the lithe, tightly muscled body astride the animal. He watched as the cold, imperious face scanned the scene, the single eagle feather rising from his browband. Hawkwing moved the pony backward, into the deeper brush again, where he had cover yet could see the entire scene in front of him.

Fargo grew the Colt from its holster. He couldn't risk waiting much longer. One of the braves could suddenly see that the women's bonds were cut or come onto one of the troopers waiting in the bushes. Surprise would be gone and with it his most important weapon. He drew his lips back as he risked waiting a few minutes more. The main force of the Crow had to be near. Their timing was too good for anything else. Dammit, he swore, as he saw two of the Crow move close to the far end of the line of stakes almost to where the five troopers lay. There was no more time to wait.

He brought the Colt up, tried to draw a bead on Hawkwing, but the Crow was too concealed in the brush. He chose one of the bucks closer, tightened his finger on the trigger. The single shot shattered the morning stillness, and he saw the force of the bullet drive the Indian face down into the soft soil. Sergeant O'Neill had been ready and waiting, Fargo smiled appreciatively as hardly ten seconds passed before the blue-clad troopers galloped out of the brush on the opposite bank, laying down a thunderous barrage. The sergeant had divided his small squad into two platoons to make it appear larger, and the second one charged out as the first peeled off. They were firing as much for effect as for accuracy, and Fargo saw the Crow warriors diving for cover. Two bucks didn't make it, and as he watched, the women dropped to the ground, almost in unison, and he knew the Crow chieftain now realized something had gone wrong.

The sergeant had already started to ford the river with his first platoon, the troops laying down a steady barrage as they rode. The Crow were shouting now, and he caught commands from Hawkwing, barely visible in the thick brush that all but covered the pony. He raised the Colt again as six warriors leaped from cover, racing for the women on the ground, bearing bone knives, tomahawks, and short hand lances made of sharpened pine branches. He fired, saw one stumble and go down spread-eagle to twitch and then lie still. He watched as the others seemed to stop in midair, turn, twist, clutch at their bodies, and all go down as the five troopers opened fire. But a dozen more near-naked figures raced for the women. He brought down another, missed one who leaped into the air. The troopers were bringing them down, but still more came running to the attack, darting and twisting to reach where the women lay. Fargo cursed aloud.

Hawkwing had ordered all his warriors to finish the captives. He was bent on denying the rescuers their victory. "Bastard," Fargo muttered aloud as he rose, fired, saw one buck throw his arms skyward, stagger forward as though suddenly drunk, and collapse on the ground. The women were screaming now, some on their feet, trying to avoid the leaping, slashing figures. Fargo ran forward, the Colt barking furiously. A young girl screamed as an Indian caught her by the hair, yanked her back, and raised his arm to plunge a heavy knife into her. Fargo fired and the buck staggered, released his hold on the girl's hair, turned to face the big man charging at him. He tried to raise the knife but fell forward, his chest shattered.

Another big buck had a woman by the throat, wrestling her to the ground. Fargo fired again and saw the Indian's head seem to leave his shoulders as the woman twisted herself away. He heard the hissing rush of air, tried to half fall, half dive to the side as the tomahawk whistled toward him. He was only partly in time as the weapon glanced along the side of his temple. He went down, the pain shooting through his head. The world started to close in on him, but he rolled, shook his head, and the curtain tore away. He saw the Crow racing at him and got the Colt up, fired from flat on his back as the Indian leaped. The shot caught the flying body through the abdomen, and Fargo rolled to one side as the Indian doubled up in midair, hit the ground with both hands clutching his stomach, a long, guttural cry escaping his lips.

Fargo rose to one knee, turned to see Sergeant O'Neill and his first platoon racing out of the river. He'd crossed almost without return fire, as Hawkwing had ordered every warrior to kill the captives. The Crow still alive were fleeing, racing for the brush and their ponies. Only a few made it as O'Neill's troopers cut down the rest. Fargo pulled himself to his feet, his eyes peering into the heavy brush back from the riverbank. The tall single eagle's feather was not in sight. Hawkwing had fled, slipped back into the heavy foliage. He was on his way downriver to cross and join his main force.

Fargo turned his glance to where the troopers had dismounted. A strange silence had returned to the riverbank, broken only by the grateful sobs of the women as the soldiers helped them to their feet. The second small platoon was in midriver with the wagon, he saw, Celia sitting beside the driver. As the wagon reached the shore he saw her leap off to embrace Judy Thompson.

"You did it, by God," Sergeant O'Neill said, cutting into his thoughts. "Most of them are alive."

"Most of them," Fargo said as his gaze took in the forms that lay crumpled and still near the stakes. He glanced up to see the woman whose bonds he'd first severed. She was coming toward him.

"God bless you, all of you," she said, "We'd pretty near given up hope. I'm Ada Cartell."

Fargo nodded, recognized the name from the list he'd been given. Her husband had died trying to recapture her. He studied her for a moment, a strong face that had known pain and hardship before. He nodded to the still forms. "Will you help me?" he asked.

"Yes, of course," she said at once and went with him to the first body. He saw her steady herself, gather inner strength she had drawn on many times before, he was certain. "Carrie Aston," she said, followed him to the second woman. "Maggie Deeds," she said, her voice toneless. "Arabelle Morgan," she said as he paused again. There was only one more, the young, buxom girl with the black eyes and the long black hair. "Rosina," the woman said. "I never knew her last name."

"Donnato," Fargo said, and the bitterness was in his voice. He felt the woman's eyes on him. "There are things she'll never know, and that's the only good in it," he said as he turned away. He saw the five troopers standing together, their eyes on him. "You did well, goddamn well," he said. "General Peterson's going to hear about it."

The sergeant's voice cut in. "We'd best get back to the others," he said.

Fargo nodded and saw Celia coming toward him leading the Ovaro. "Thanks," he said as he took the horse from her. "It's not over," he said.

"I know," she answered, her eyes round. "But I'll still be waiting."

He patted her cheek and climbed onto the pinto. The sergeant had detailed a burial party and four troopers to stay with the wagon. Most of the women were already climbing inside it, he saw, and he wheeled the pinto around, waved an arm into the air, and was in a fast canter as he splashed into the river. The sergeant came up beside him when they reached the other side. He glanced back. The line of troopers rode in a tight column. Miraculously, they hadn't lost a man. He glimpsed the wagon starting across the river and returned his attention to hard riding. The passage between the rocks was less than a mile away when he heard the sound of gunfire.

His thoughts raced almost as fast as the pinto's flying hooves. The Crow had two things turn sour. They weren't ones to dig in and fight against the odds. That wasn't the way of the Indian. They were essentially raiders. Strike, pillage, and run. If the odds were too great, leave and find another time, another way to strike again. Hawkwing had added his own twists to their ways, but he hadn't changed the basics. The sound of the gunfire grew louder quickly, cutting into his thoughts.

"You have a bugler in this squad, sergeant?" he asked.

"Just so happens we do, sir," the sergeant said.

"Then tell him to start blowing that horn. Tell him to blow it hard. We'll make them think the Seventh Regiment is on the way," Fargo said as he bent low in the saddle and sent the pinto into a full gallop.

The sergeant barked commands and a moment later the sound of the bugle filled the rushing wind, the repeated tattoo of notes that formed the signature of the U.S. Cavalry. The road dipped, then rose and dipped again. As he reached the top of the rise, the scene before him came into view. The passageway between the rocks was strewn with lifeless Crow bodies. The ambush had been highly successful, but the lieutenant's troopers were still behind the rocks and now the remaining Crow fired down on them from higher ground. Fargo's eyes swept the rocks, seeking one figure, finally spying him astride his pony on a high, flat rock, directing his warriors with hand signals. He saw Hawkwing turn toward him as he swept into sight with the troopers.

The Crow chieftain spurred the pony forward at once, leaped from the flat rock to a lower one, and then disappeared from sight behind a tall side of stone. But Fargo saw the other Indians begin to scramble down from their vantage points, heading for their ponies waiting below. "You take the right side, I'll take the left," he called to the sergeant as he veered off with half of the column following. He drew the big Sharps rifle from its saddle holster, fired from the full gallop, and saw his shot wing a painted buck leaping down from the rocks. The Indian fell the rest of the way clutching his shoulder, landed on the ground to lie still for a moment. He rose as he saw the pinto thundering toward him, drew a heavy-bladed hunting knife from a deerskin sheath attached to his breechclout thong. Fargo smashed the heavy butt of the rifle into his face as he started to leap upward. The Crow fell backward, red breaking from his face in a half-dozen places. But he still rose to his feet as Fargo turned the pinto around, the knife still in his hand.

Fargo prodded the pinto forward and headed for the man, then caught the shadow over his head, knew better than to try to look up. He dived from the saddle and the Indian struck him across the hips as he dived from the rock above. Fargo gasped in pain as the combination of weight and momentum smashed into him. He hit the ground rolling forward, continued rolling, and came up on one knee. The Indian that had plunged onto him lay on the ground, starting to pull himself together, but Fargo saw the other Crow, his face a bloody mask of broken bone and torn flesh, rushing at him with the bone knife ready to strike. Fargo raised the Colt and fired, heard the hammer click on an empty chamber. He flung himself to one side and the Crow plunged past him, stumbled, and fell.

Fargo's powerful leg muscles kicked out, his boot smashing into the Indian's head. The man fell to his side, and Fargo brought the barrel of the heavy Colt onto the Indian's skull with all his strength. The Crow's body went limp as Fargo heard his skull crack. He swung around to see the Crow that had leaped on him. The Indian came at him, half-dazed, yet his hands reaching out to find his enemy's throat. Fargo brushed the man aside and crashed the Colt against his forehead, stepped back as the Crow pitched onto his face, shuddered, and lay still.

Fargo pulled himself straight and winced, but his eyes swept the rocks. The Crow had mostly fled, a few still giving battle with their pursuers. But he sought only one figure, and suddenly he saw the lithe form in the distance, the lone eagle feather unmistakable. The Crow chief was holding a trooper, a knife at the soldier's throat. Fargo swung onto the pinto, spurred the horse forward, and slipped shells into the Colt. He fired, Hawkwing still far away, and saw the shot miss. But the Crow looked up, saw him coming. He dropped his hold on the soldier and vaulted onto his pony, raced out of sight behind the rocks. Fargo galloped after him, turned up the narrow passageway where the Crow had vanished. He came out onto a small plateau, a half-dozen passages through the rocks to his right. He slowed, eyes narrowed, guided the pinto to the side of the rock and away from the open area. The Colt in hand, he guided the pinto through the nearest opening between the rocks, moving carefully. He emerged onto another small flat area where more rocks tumbled jaggedly together and led downward.

He swore under his breath. Hawkwing had vanished. The Indian had elected to flee rather than confront him. He would have had the advantage of surprise and position, Fargo mused. Yet he turned away. Fargo guided the pinto back down the way he'd come, still thinking about Hawkwing's actions, and found himself mildly disturbed by them. When he emerged at the base of the rocks he found the young trooper leaning against a tall rock, his face still ashen.

"Thank you, sir," the trooper said, looking up at him.

"A close one," Fargo remarked.

"Too close. I thought I was done for," the trooper said. "I would have been, but he was asking me questions. He speaks enough English."

"Questions?" Fargo frowned. "What kind of questions?"

"About you, sir."

"Me?" Fargo echoed.

"He asked who the big man was with eyes like a morning lake," the trooper said. "He said he'd cut my throat if I didn't answer. I told him you were called Fargo."

Fargo's eyes narrowed. Hawkwing's actions took on added meaning now. He'd refused a confrontation because he wanted more than surprise and position. He wanted revenge. He turned the pinto and started back to the others. "Get yourself together and rejoin your squad, soldier," he said to the trooper as he rode on. He reached the passageway between the rocks again, picked his way through the litter of bodies, more than enough wearing blue, he noted grimly. He found Lieutenant Smith standing alone against a slab of tall stone. His young eyes would never be truly young again, Fargo saw. He dismounted, and Smith looked at him for a long moment.

"You were right all along," Smith said slowly. "We'd

have been slaughtered. It was bad enough with us doing the surprising."

"Bad enough," Fargo agreed, glancing across the passageway strewn with bodies. A sergeant came up to Smith, offered a weary salute.

"I'll organize a burial detail, sir?" he said, and Smith nodded. Fargo glanced across the passageway and saw the wagon rolling down toward him, Celia beside the driver again, the four troopers riding escort gazing with shock at the scene of carnage. He stepped forward as the wagon rolled to a halt, and Celia swung to the ground, ran into his arms.

"My God. Oh, my God," she breathed. She clung to him for another moment, then pushed away and her eyes found Smith. "My uncle?" she asked.

"He's still alive, but he's in a bad way," the lieutenant said. "He took three Crow arrows through the chest. This way, ma'am." Fargo followed as Smith led Celia behind a rock where Colonel Kaster sat propped up, the front of his uniform more red than blue. His colorless eyes were half-open, managed to open wider as he focused on Celia. "I gave him his gun when the fighting started," the lieutenant said. "He leaped up and tried to take command. I tried to stop him, but I couldn't. He yelled for the men to follow him, and he ran past the rocks. He didn't run far."

"It was his pride," Celia said.

The lieutenant's glance touched Fargo. "He was drunk, ma'am," Smith said softly but firmly. "It was liquor, not pride."

Fargo watched the fleeting shadow of pain cross Celia's face. Truth left no hiding places. She knelt down beside the man as his mouth worked, a rasping wheeze escaping his lips. "Tell Martha I did it," the colonel gasped. "Tell her I did it the way she wanted me to. I led the attack."

Celia glanced at Fargo, and he felt the crease dig into

his brow. "The way she wanted you to?" he asked, bending low to the man.

The colonel's watery eyes blinked in agreement. "She told me to go after him. 'Lead them into battle,' she said. 'You can do it.' " The man's voice became a sputter, then a long wheezing sound. Fargo took Celia by the elbow, pulled her to her feet, and led her away. He heard the man's last rasping rattle of breath as he turned the corner of rock to the other side. Celia leaned against him in silence, and he let her stay until she finally pulled away. Her eyes met his, a kind of searching to salvage small triumphs in their depths.

"That cuts Martha off that list of those who could have sent the four killers after you," she said.

"Maybe," he allowed.

"Maybe?" Celia flared. "Of course it does. You said if the colonel died she'd have only a measly widow's pension. You told me yourself she wanted to keep him alive as an investment."

"Maybe," he said again.

"Dammit, that's not fair. Can't you admit when you're wrong?" she accused.

"I will, when I'm wrong," he said.

"And when will that be?" Celia asked with tartness.

"Another time, another place," he said. "Now get your little ass back on the wagon. I've other things to think about."

She turned away, annoyed, and he watched her go back to the wagon and the other women. He judged it would take most of the day for the burial detail to finish, and he took the pinto and rode back along the passageway until it widened. He halted, let his eyes slowly scan the land as he turned thoughts in his mind, came up with nothing that satisfied. He turned as he heard the horse approaching from behind him and saw the lieutenant.

148

"Another hour or so and we'll be ready to move on," Smith said. His eyes followed Fargo's gaze out across the slopes and forests. "All of it done with and he still got away," Smith said bitterly.

"Not far away," Fargo said. "He's out there, waiting, thinking, planning."

"Or just running," the lieutenant said.

"No," Fargo answered and saw the lieutenant's eyes questioning his definiteness. "He knows I was the one. He knows I stopped the colonel from playing into his hands. He had it all his way till then," Fargo said. "It's a personal thing, now. He wants his revenge."

"Killing you?" Smith said.

"He wants that, but he wants more," Fargo said.

"Such as?"

Fargo's lips drew back. "I don't know, but something more," he answered. "The women, maybe."

"The women?" the lieutenant echoed.

"It'd be salvaging something to him," Fargo said. "It started with his taking them. He failed at cheating us out of saving them. They could be a last victory out of all that went wrong."

"I'll put an extra detail to guard the wagon," Smith said. He turned back and rode away while Fargo waited, his gaze continuing to sweep the land while the tightness inside him grew tighter. He finally rode back to rejoin the others and arrived just as the lieutenant finished a short service for the fallen. Smith handed him a package wrapped in the regimental flag. "The colonel's sidearm and his personal possessions," he said. "I thought you might like to give them to Mrs. Kaster."

Fargo took the package and put it into his saddlebag. They had a few hours of daylight still left, and the lieutenant decided to take advantage of them. He moved the remainder of his troops forward, and Fargo noted he had half the soldiers riding with the wagon. Some of the women rode on extra horses beside the wagon, and he saw Celia on her bay beside Judy Thompson.

When night came and they made camp, he bedded down away from the others, on the side of a hillock, his bedroll hidden under the low leaves of a hackenberry. He was almost asleep when he heard the footsteps, tentative, searching footsteps, and he sat up, the Colt in his hand. He saw the figure, the wheat hair silvery in the night. "Dammit, what are you doing up here?" he asked in a whisper.

She turned at his voice, hurried to him, and sank onto the bedroll, her arms around him. "Just hold me," she said, clinging to him. He let her stay against him and then pushed her back.

"You can't stay," he told her gently.

She peered at his intense handsomeness. "It's Hawkwing, isn't it?" she said. "You're waiting for him to come after you."

His shrug was an admission. "Go back to the wagon," he said even as he wondered where she'd be in most danger, with him or with the women. Perhaps there was little difference, he reflected. He stood up with her, and she returned to the wagon with him in troubled silence, clung for another long moment before going past the row of troopers. Fargo went back to his bedroll and finally slept, the light sleep of the mountain lion, every sense ready to spring into alertness.

But the night passed quietly, and he rejoined the column when morning came. The return to Sunwater took three days of steady riding, and each day Fargo rode apart from the troopers, sometimes ahead, sometimes behind, sometimes in a wide circle around the slower-moving column. He found no sign of the Indian chief, yet he knew the Crow was there, watching, following, his presence as real as though he were visible.

Yet the days passed with only the growing excitement of the women as they drew nearer to their families. As they halted to let the horses drink at a waterhole, the lieutenant sought out Fargo. "We'll be in Sunwater by night," he said. "I think you were wrong about Hawkwing. He's off somewhere licking his wounds."

Fargo's eyes swept the horizon as he listened to the lieutenant's words. The past days made it impossible to deny the conclusion. "I hope you're right," he said.

"But you still don't think so," Smith prodded.

Fargo uttered a grim laugh. "He's out there, following, watching."

"There's no place for him to attack the wagon between here and Sunwater," the lieutenant said and again Fargo had to admit the reality of his words. "Maybe he has been following, but he couldn't find the right moment to strike or he decided we had the women too tightly protected."

Fargo nodded. It was another possibility he couldn't deny. But he knew the Crow. The spirit of revenge refused being put aside, and the uneasiness continued to ride with him as they moved on, Sunwater but a few hours away. Night descended on the column as Celia brought the bay alongside him.

"I understand the lieutenant is bringing everyone into the compound and sent out riders to notify the families," she said.

"That's right," Fargo answered. "They'll come in fast. The reunion won't take more than an hour or two."

"I want to tell Martha about Uncle Henry," Celia said.

He shrugged. "That's fine with me," he told her.

"Are you ready to admit that Martha is off that list of yours?" Celia asked.

"Maybe," Fargo said, his face as expressionless as his voice.

"You're a funny one, Fargo." Celia half laughed. "You've got to learn when to back off."

"I'll work on it," he said tonelessly.

"I'll be waiting when you're ready, Fargo," Celia said softly, and wheeled the bay away. Fargo returned his eyes to the night, but nothing moved across the relatively flat land. When the dark outline of Fort Jasper came into sight, Lieutenant Smith rode up beside him.

"We made it, Fargo, whatever the reasons," he said.

"Whatever the reasons," Fargo echoed, and the grimness still stayed with him. "Celia's going to tell Martha Kaster, and you'll be plenty busy for the next hour or so. I'll come visit tomorrow," he said.

The lieutenant nodded, and Fargo spurred the pinto forward as the column turned into the compound. He paused to watch the wagon enter, the last troops following behind it. They had indeed made it, and he felt good for that. He turned the pinto and slowly rode to the rooming house, dismounted, and felt the tiredness in his body. Patty was in the small foyer as he entered, her gray-blue eyes round. She just stared at him for a moment and then flew into his arms, clung to him. She searched his face when she finally stepped back.

"You look like a man that needs nothing but sleep," she said.

"You hit the bull's-eye," he said. She opened the door to his room, waited a moment as he dropped his gear on the floor and sank onto the bed.

"Sleep tight," she said as she closed the door. Fargo lay for a moment and then rose, undressed, and stretched his long, tired body across the bed. He was asleep in moments, shaking away the uneasiness that insisted on still clinging to him. He slept, exhaustion and a sense of security inside the house combining to let him sleep deeply. He didn't know how long he'd been asleep when he heard the scream, Patty's voice, terror and pain. He bolted from the bed in shorts, grabbing his gunbelt as he ran from the room. Patty screamed again, but this time the scream ended in a gargled sound and then abrupt silence. Cursing, he ran down the hall to her room at the other end, flung the door open, the Colt in his hand.

"Ah, Jesus, Jesus," he moaned. Patty lay across her bed, her naked, slender body covered with blood. She had been gored from abdomen to chest and her throat sliced open. He stood for a moment, overwhelmed by helplessness and anguish. There'd be no turning back clocks anymore for Patty Rooney. He stared at the open window behind her. He seemed to stand there for an eternity, but it was only seconds as the anguish turned to rage, total, absolute, consuming rage.

He leaped through the open window, dropped to one knee as his eyes scanned the ground. He saw the blood at once, Patty's blood. The Crow had come on foot and he was fleeing on foot, his pony waiting someplace not too far away. Fargo, in shorts and gunbelt, raced around the corner of the house and vaulted onto the pinto, returned to follow the trail of spattered blood. As he rode, the picture formed itself, all too clear now. The Crow had followed all along, watched, lain low, continued to follow as the column went into the fort. He'd probably been on foot by then, Fargo cursed, had watched him go to Patty's house. He had simply waited, edged in closer, circled behind the houses as the crowds gathered at the fort for the reunion. He'd waited again, waited for the night to grow deep.

Fargo reined up, saw the blood spots go into a thicket behind the single row of houses that formed the main street of Sunwater. He parted the bushes, saw the prints of the Indian pony as the Crow had raced away. But he had only a minute's start, and Fargo sent the pinto into a full gallop. He cursed into the wind as he raced the horse through the night, cursed at himself, at the world, and at the relentless savagery of the Crow. The rage consuming him rose higher to obliterate all feelings but hate, total, naked hate, a savagery to meet savagery.

He was cursing aloud as he caught sight of the Indian pony. The lithe figure on the horse turned to see him, and he saw Hawkwing rein up, leap from the saddle, tomahawk in hand. He darted into a cluster of trees, and Fargo dived from the pinto before it came to a halt. He moved into the trees, the Colt in his hand, halted, every muscle tensed, his ears straining. He caught the faint movement of a branch, then the hiss of air, and he whirled, his hand going up to protect himself. The tomahawk crashed against the Colt, knocking the gun from his grip. He heard both weapons fall into the brush, but he'd no time to find them as the Crow emerged, a wide-bladed hunting knife in his hand. He saw the insane triumph in the man's face, his lips forming a gargoyle parody of a smile.

"Your woman," he said.

"No, you goddamn savage sonofabitch," Fargo said. "But you'll pay just the same."

Hawkwing let out a shout, dived forward, slicing at the big man with a knife. Fargo saw the blood-smeared blade and his rage exploded into uncaring hatred. He rushed at the Crow, pulled away from an upward thrust of the knife, brought one big hand down on the Indian's forearm, the other on his elbow. He twisted and the Crow gasped in pain as he dropped the knife. Fargo released his grip, spun the man around, and smashed a sledgehammer blow into his face. The Crow fell backward, managed to roll aside as Fargo tried to bring his foot down onto his neck. He rolled again, came up on his feet, and tried to retrieve the knife. Fargo rushed in, smashed another blow to the man's head. Hawkwing staggered sideways but kept his feet as Fargo scooped up the knife.

The Crow lunged forward, tried to grasp hold of the weapon, but Fargo swiped sideways with the blade. Hawkwing's lithe, tightly muscled body managed to twist away. Fargo came in again and the Crow began to twist away again as Fargo started another side sweep with the blade but suddenly changed to a forward thrust. He rammed the knife into the Crow's belly, driving it deep, and enjoyed the way the man's eyes bulged. He was cursing wildly as he pulled the blade free and sliced upward with it, almost cutting the Indian in two as he drew the knife from his crotch to his throat. The man's body seemed to come apart as his innards spilled out.

"Bastard. Rotten bastard," Fargo cursed wildly as he plunged the blade into the Crow again and again. "For Patty, you fucking sonofabitch," he shouted. "Bastard, stinkin' bastard." Finally he fell back, his breath coming in long, harsh drafts. Fargo stared at the object on the ground in front of him, nothing more than a carcass now, a dismembered, disemboweled, bloodied carcass. Slowly, he rose to his feet, dropped the knife onto the thing staining the ground, and turned away. He was still cursing softly as he rode the pinto back to town.

He had tried to think as the Crow, see as the Crow, act as the Crow. He had succeeded and he had failed and perhaps the difference lay somewhere in between. But it was over now, all but one thing.

•

8

Morning came in gray and bitter. Some said the sun was out. Fargo disagreed. He'd done all that had to be done at the house and spoken to Lieutenant Smith, who had promised a proper burial. There was only one thing left to do, and Fargo walked across the compound with the flag-wrapped package in his hand. He glimpsed Celia at the window of her quarters as she watched his slow steps to the colonel's office.

Martha opened the door for him, closed it when he stepped into the small office. Wordlessly, he handed her the package, his face stone. She put the package on the desk and unwrapped it. She stared at the big army-issue Dragoon Colt, the wallet and keychain beside it, finally lifted pained eyes to Fargo. "Will you be staying on some?" she asked.

He shook his head. "No. I've a report to give General Peterson and a few things to set straight in it," he said.

A tiny frown touched Martha Kaster's forehead. "Such as?" she inquired.

"He didn't die a hero's death. Fact is, he'd been relieved of his command," Fargo said and watched her black eyes grow smaller.

"For God's sake, Fargo, let the man be. Let things

stand the way they are. He was in command. Why do you want to smear the man's name?" she said.

"Truth, that's why. Truth," Fargo shot back. "He's not going down in the record book as a hero when he was a drunken sot who would've led his men to slaughter." He turned, started for the door.

"No, I won't let you do that," he heard Martha shout. He turned to see her holding the big Dragoon Colt on him. "I'll kill you if you do that," she said.

He let surprise touch his face. "You'd kill me to save the colonel's reputation?" he asked.

"Yes," she said righteously, keeping the revolver on him.

"How touching, Martha," Fargo said. "Only it's not his reputation you give a shit about, except as how it affects you."

She frowned. "What are you talking about?"

"You know damn well what I'm talking about," Fargo threw back. "You keep making mistakes, Martha, like hiring those gunslingers to kill me. That was when you were afraid I'd show up the colonel and he'd commit suicide on you and leave you with that measly widow's pension. That's when you thought if you got rid of me it'd keep the colonel alive and drawing his pay. Your second mistake was telling the poor slob to go out and be a hero, knowing he'd get himself killed."

"If I were interested in keeping him alive why would I urge him to get himself killed?" Martha Kaster sneered.

Fargo's smile was coldly tolerant. "Things changed. I came back. Your hired help didn't do the job right. Then he tricked me into telling him where the camp was and had me clapped into jail. He insisted on riding into the lion's den, so you had to do a fast switch. You egged him on to go out and get himself killed, gave him a real pep talk. And we both know why, don't we, Martha?" Fargo said. "I remembered when he said how you'd told him to lead the way into battle. If he died a hero in combat the army'd pay his full salary as pension." He paused, smiled again at the woman as her eyes glistened coldly. "It all comes out the same way—keep him alive by getting rid of me or egging him on to kill himself in battle, whichever would keep that full pay rolling in to you. But it's not going to work, Martha. He's not going to be a hero and you're not going to draw a hero's pension."

Fargo turned from her again and started for the door. "You bastard," she shouted. "I'll kill you."

He paused, looked back at her. She had the arm revolver leveled at him, holding it with both hands. "You wouldn't get away with it, Martha," he said.

"I'll say it was an accident, the gun just went off. They'll believe a hero's grieving widow," she snarled.

"Go to hell, Martha," he said and continued toward the door. He halted as he heard the metallic clicks of empty chambers being fired. He turned, drew his hand from his pocket. The four bullets were in his palm. "I took the precaution of taking them out," he said. "That's twice you tried and failed. Give up, Martha. Start figuring out how you'll live on that measly widow's pension."

He pulled the door open and strode outside to see Celia waiting. She read the harsh lines of his face and let the question die on her lips. She fell into step beside him. "What are you going to do?" she asked.

"Work my way back to General Peterson. But first I'm going to forget the world for a little while," he said, his voice hard.

"How?" she asked.

"By drinking and screwing," he flung at her, halted, pulled her around to face him. "Want to come?" he asked.

The wheat hair nodded vigorously. "Just let me get my

things," she said. "I'll only be a minute." She ran off, her little round rear bobbing with promise.

"Hurry up. I don't want to waste one fucking minute," he murmured softly and meant every literal word of it.

LOOKING FORWARD!

The following is the opening section
from the next novel in the exciting
Trailsman series from Signet:

The Trailsman #15:
THE STALKING HORSE

*The Colorado Territory,
where the Arikaree River ran
south from the corner of Nebraska
and the land was made
of heaven and hell.*

It had begun, as it so often does, over a girl. But not the usual way. The girl was just an excuse, a convenient pawn. The three men had been looking for one. Fargo had become convinced of as much during the past two days. It was but a matter of time before they found one that suited them. Skye Fargo smiled inwardly. Coming to the dancehall had been almost offering them the chance they wanted. And he'd done so on purpose. And now he took the girl by the wrist, a firm but gentle touch, started to move her to one side.

The tallest of the three men uttered a growling protest at once. "Leave her where she is, mister," he ordered.

Fargo's lake-blue eyes, cold as blue ice floes now,

bored into the man as he continued to move the girl to the side.

"Goddamn, you hear me, mister?" the man barked.

The girl now safely out of the line of fire, Fargo's hand dropped down to rest along the side of his thigh, inches from the big Colt .45 on his hip. "I'd hate to put a bullet through somebody I don't even know," he said almost apologetically.

"You've a big mouth, mister," the man said.

"And you've been following me around ever since I got here two days ago. Why?" Fargo said.

"You're crazy," the man snapped back, and out of the corner of his eye, Fargo saw the others in the dancehall moving to the sides, taking cover behind bare wood round tables. "The girl's going with us," the man growled.

"Not unless it's to your funeral," Fargo said mildly.

"We've got three guns, mister," the man said.

"I can count," Fargo remarked. He read the stab of uneasiness that came into the man's eyes. The man was suddenly uncertain whether he was up against a colossal bluff or the kind of gunhand he'd no stomach to face. Fargo grunted silently. He'd tabled the trio the minute he'd seen them watching him. They called him the Trailsman because he was the best, and reading men was not that different from reading a trail. These three were drifters, scroungers. It was there to see in so many ways—gunbelts of cracked leather because of not enough saddle soap, boots given little care, shirts that didn't fit right because they were begged, borrowed, or stolen. And the small meanness in their faces that was part of those who scrounged their way through the world.

The man broke the long moment of silence. "Go for your gun, mister. We like to give a man a chance," he said.

"You're real sports. You first," Fargo said.

Again, he saw the uneasiness fill the man's eyes, watched his tongue flick across suddenly dry lips. Fargo's glance passed over the other two. They were no more filled with confidence and waited to follow the taller one's lead.

"You'd be nothin' but a sitting duck, and we don't shoot sitting ducks," the man said. "You're lucky we're that way, mister."

"I guess so," Fargo said and watched the man turn, gesture to the others to follow as he strode from the dancehall. Fargo's eyes stayed on them till they disappeared out the swinging doors. He nodded to the girl, and she came alongside him as he went to the bar. A murmur of voices came to life again as people began to move out from behind tables. The bartender, a stocky, gray-haired man with a not unpleasant face that nonetheless carried shrewdness in it, appraised him as he halted at the bar. His eyes took in the powerfully built frame of the big man, the lake-blue eyes in the intense, chiseled face, the sense of latent hair-trigger acuteness in the man.

"If you were bluffing, you won, mister," the bartender said with admiration.

"If I was bluffing." Fargo smiled.

"If you weren't, it was still three to one," the bartender said.

"Three scroungers," Fargo spat out contemptuously.

"Either way, this drink's on the house," the bartender said.

Fargo's eyes went to the girl, thin, pretty in a sad way, pale-blue eyes that weren't in keeping with the cheap dress and overly rouged cheeks. "What's your pleasure, Carrie?" he asked.

"Beer," she said, and he nodded at the bartender.

"Yours?" the man asked.

"Bourbon," Fargo said, and the bartender poured him a shot glass of good Kentucky brew. Fargo downed the drink. "Another. I'm paying this time," he said. The bartender refilled his glass, his eyes still studying the big man. Fargo carefully placed the glass in the center of the bar. "You've a back way out of here?" he asked.

"Sure," the bartender said. "But you just ordered your bourbon."

"I'll be back for it," he said. He stepped away from the bar and walked to the back of the dancehall. The incident had been no victory, despite what others took it to be. The three drifters were easily rattled, unwilling to risk taking on more than they felt they could handle. But they were no less dangerous for it. Like all coyotes, they'd backed off only to give themselves a better chance. They were waiting for him to come out later, overconfident, perhaps drunk. They'd do their job then, the easy way. He let a long sigh escape him. They were always the same, the small-minded cowards for hire, their thinking and their actions completely predictable. They'd gun him down without a second thought, and he'd offer them no more. But why, he wondered. They hadn't chosen him out of a clear blue sky. Maybe he could save one to question.

He slowly opened the back door of the dancehall, slipped into the night outside. His back pressed against the outer wall, he made his way along the back of the structure, edged around the corner where he faced the side of the buildings across the street. His eyes traveled slowly along the structures, halted at the general store that faced the dancehall, windows darkened now, an overhang deepening the shadows in front of it. His eyes narrowed, strained, and focused on the dark bulk in one corner of the porch-like entranceway, two figures squatted down. He let his gaze move slowly to the left, found the third figure in the other corner. As he watched, one of them lighted a cigarette and he caught the dull glint of gunmetal.

They had settled down for a long wait, their eyes on the entrance of the dancehall, a half-circle of light on the dark street. He drew the Colt, raised it, paused as a cut-under coal wagon passed with its high rear wheels. The wagon rolled on, and Fargo saw the flicker of the cigarette. It was as good a target as anything. He sighted along the heavy barrel of the Colt, fired, two shots so fast they sounded almost as one. He saw the glow of the cigarette sail into the air, the guttural half-gasp, the two forms pitch forward as if tied together. His eyes and the Colt had moved but a fraction to the right where the third figure half rose.

"Drop the gun," Fargo said. "Give me some answers and you can walk away."

The reply was a shot, and Fargo heard the bullet slam into the wall a foot from where he crouched. He fired as the figure started to race away. The man fell forward from the two steps that led to the general store, landed face down on the ground, pulled himself to his knees and fell forward again. He lay motionless this time. No answers, Fargo grunted as he holstered the Colt and returned to the dancehall through the rear door.

The exchange of shots had been easily heard inside the dancehall, and as he came back inside through the rear entrance he saw the eyes that followed him as he went to the bar. He picked up the shot glass, nodded to the bartender, and smiled at the girl as he downed the bourbon. He saw the bartender watching him with a mixture of uncertainty and curiosity.

"Some ambushes work, some don't," Fargo remarked

casually and saw the curiosity in the man's eyes turn to a kind of respectful admiration. Fargo turned to the girl. "Ready?" he asked.

Her pale-blue eyes held his gaze. "You don't have to," she said, and he frowned back. "You didn't come here for a girl. You didn't pick me out. You just took up with me because you knew those men would start something."

He smiled in admission. There was hurt in her voice, sensitivity still part of her. He liked that. "A man's got a right to change his mind," he said. She studied him a moment more, and he caught the tiny hint of pleased satisfaction that came into her eyes. She turned, took his hand, and led him up the stairs to a small, neat room.

"Why did those men come on like that?" she asked as he sat down on the edge of the single bed with the brass ends.

"I don't know. You ever see them before?" he returned.

"No, but I've only been here a few days. I'm new at this. Madame Charlene's sort of trying me out," the girl said, and Fargo smiled inwardly. The answer explained a lot of things about her.

"I didn't notice Madame Charlene downstairs," he said.

"She went away for a few days," Carrie said as she slipped out of the cheap dress to stand before him only in pink pantie-drawers. She pushed them down, and stepped out of them, and he took a moment to enjoy the sight of her. A thin girl, her ribs showing, she had long, thin legs, a small, curly triangle, and breasts to match, rounded little mounds with unexpectedly large deep-pink tips. He felt sorry for her. There was a somewhat waiflike quality to her, and she'd little that would keep her or Madame Charlene happy and wealthy. For the most part, the men who came to dancehalls wanted the overflowing, lush girls with bodies that shouted earthy sex.

"You going to stay all dressed?" she asked, her eyes wide as she came to sink down on the bed. He laughed, stood up, and shed clothes, suddenly finding himself attracted to the thin, somehow needing little creature. He saw Carrie's eyes grow wide as he shed shorts, came toward her. "Oh, Jeez," she breathed, and he watched her lips come up. She reached up, drew him to her, and suddenly she was quivering, fastening herself to him, pulling and caressing, the small breasts little soft spots against his chest.

He took one large nipple in his mouth and pulled on it. "Ah, ah . . . Jeez . . ." she breathed, and her long, thin legs fell open. "Come inside . . . oh, Christ, come inside," she gasped. He pushed his powerful, pulsating organ into her, and her entire body quivered and trembled with fervor. Carrie exploded almost at once around him, and her mouth pressed against his ear. "Stay . . . stay . . . I'll be ready again in a minute," she gasped. "I'm like that."

She was indeed like that, he discovered, coming again and again with quivering intensity. Finally as she lay beside him, drawing in deep breaths, he found himself surprised again at how much steel-wire sexuality thin, small-busted girls possessed. It was something he had reflected upon before, but it continued to surprise him each time.

He stood up, began to dress, and let his eyes enjoy her thin, waiflike body. There was an attractiveness to her naked, he saw, but he had long ago come to appreciate that beauty came in many ways. She would still be passed over by most men who came to Madame Charlene's dancehall.

"Will you come back?" she asked, sitting up as he finished dressing and put the silver dollar on the small dresser.

"Not likely," he said and saw the expression touch her face at once. He cupped her chin in his hand. "Nothing to do with you," he said quickly. "For someone new at this you do very well."

"I'm not new at doing it, just at getting paid for it," she said defensively.

"Good luck," he said. She rose, was beside him as he reached the door.

"I'm glad you were the first one here," she said.

He patted her naked, thin little rump. "Maybe I will be back," he told her and slipped out the door. He went downstairs, paused at the bar.

"Sheriff Barker was here asking about the three dead men outside," the bartender said. "Nobody here saw anything."

"That's right," Fargo said.

"What are you doing here, mister?" the man asked.

"Came here to talk to somebody about a job," Fargo said. "Young woman wants to hire me to find her father." Fargo's hand touched the letter in his pocket as he spoke.

The bartender's eyes grew smaller as he stopped polishing the glass in his hand, stared at the big man in front of him. "Her name wouldn't be Caldwell, would it?" he asked slowly.

Fargo's brows lifted a fraction. "It would," he said. "Got anything you can tell me?"

"I sure do," the bartender said. "I'd light out of here and not come back, mister."